MW00952698

J. N. Chaney

www.jnchaney.com

1st Edition

BOOKS BY J.N. CHANEY

The Variant Saga:

The Amber Project

Transient Echoes

Hope Everlasting

The Vernal Memory

Renegade Star Series:

Renegade Star

Renegade Atlas

Renegade Moon

Renegade Lost

Renegade Fleet

Renegade Earth

Renegade Dawn

Renegade Children

Renegade Union (Jan 2019)

Renegade Empire (March 2019)

Renegade Universe:

Nameless

Orion Colony

Orion Uncharted

Orion Awakened (Jan 2019)

Standalone Books:

Their Solitary Way

The Other Side of Nowhere

STAY UP TO DATE

Chaney posts updates, official art, previews, and other awesome stuff on his website. You can also follow him on Instagram, Facebook, and Twitter.

Search for **JN Chaney's Renegade Readers** on Facebook to join the group where readers can come together and share their lives and interests, especially regarding Chaney's books.

For updates about new releases, as well as exclusive promotions, sign up for the VIP mailing list. Head there now to receive a free copy of *The Other Side of Nowhere.*

https://www.subscribepage.com/organic

Enjoying the series? Help others discover the Variant Saga by leaving a review on Amazon.

RENEGADE LOST

BOOK 4 IN THE RENEGADE STAR SERIES

J.N. CHANEY

BOOK DESCRIPTION

Renegade Lost
Renegade Star Series #4

A lost ship. An unknown civilization.

The *Renegade Star* is stranded, its engines totally shot, surrounded by the unknown. Floating in the dead of space, they receive a strange transmission from a nearby planet, warning them to stay away or face the consequences.

When the message mentions how this world belongs to Earth, the lost cradle of humanity, Captain Jace Hughes knows he has no choice but to investigate.

Too bad this planet is a deathtrap.

With an endless snowstorm, bloodthirsty animals around every corner, and no sign of any colonies or people, the mission won't be an easy one.

Good thing they sent in the Renegade.

Experience a sprawling galactic tale in this fourth entry to *The Renegade Star* series. If you're a fan of *Firefly, Battlestar Galactica,* or *Leviathan Wakes,* you'll love this epic, space opera thriller.

CONTENTS

For my father,
Who taught me how to work

1

"Entering atmosphere," informed Sigmond. "Prepare for mild turbulence."

I sat in the cockpit, watching as the *Renegade Star* entered the upper stratosphere of an unknown planet in the middle of nowhere. Had the circumstances been different, I might have passed this planet up altogether. It was covered in snow and ice, and seemed to have nothing of any real value on its surface.

But I'd just received a transmission with a warning to stay away, because this world belonged to Earth, the lost homeworld of humanity, a place that I had once believed to be a children's bedtime story. That was before I met Abigail, Lex, Freddie, and Athena…before I discovered a portable moon that could double as a superweapon. I'd seen more evidence for the existence of Earth in the last few days to completely rewrite the history books. Not that I'd ever want that job. I wasn't a scholar or a historian. I had little interest in changing the state of the galaxy or what anyone believed. I was just a Renegade, trying to survive, trying to keep my crew alive.

As my ship continued its descent, I heard the door to the cockpit slide open behind me. Abigail came rushing in. "Why are we going down to the planet?" she asked.

She must have seen the atmosphere through the window and gotten concerned. I couldn't blame her confusion. I'd made a last-minute decision to investigate the transmission, not bothering to run any of this by her. "Take a seat," I said, gesturing with my hand. "We have a situation."

She sat down, not bothering with an argument, and stared at the holo image on the dash, which showed the terrain layout of the entire continent.

"Listen to this," I said, tapping the console. I replayed the transmission, leaning back in my seat. The mysterious woman's voice filled the cockpit. "Attention, this world is the property of Earth. All Transient vessels should avoid orbit or risk defense network capabilities, per the established colonization agreement."

Abigail's eyes widened as she turned to me. "Is this real?" she asked.

"Seems that way," I said, cutting the transmission. "We'll find out soon."

"Or we won't," she countered. "That woman is probably dead, don't you think? We might be heading down there for nothing."

"You want me to turn this ship around?" I asked, already knowing her answer.

She went quiet for a moment, but then shook her head. "No. Let's see what this is."

I nodded, satisfied with that. Abby was no fool. Anything involving Earth was worth exploring, no matter how futile it might seem. We both understood that. If *Titan* never came back for us, which was certainly a possibility, we'd have to find our own way out of here. Maybe there were answers on this planet. Maybe we could locate some parts to fix our engine. Either way, sitting in space and waiting for a rescue wasn't an option. Not for us. We weren't the sit-and-wait kind of folk.

The snowstorm picked up as we broke through the clouds and grew closer to the surface. My windows began accumulating frost so quickly I thought we might be buried before we touched the ground.

By the time we landed, the winds had picked up considerably, and I knew we'd have to wait this out before we began our investigation.

I let out a heavy sigh. "Guess we're waiting," I muttered, thumbing my Foxy Stardust bobblehead and watching it bounce. "Best we get some rest for now. Gods know I need it."

THE SCENT from the coffee machine filled the lounge with a rich aroma that made me want to smile.

I poured a cup and took a whiff of the delicious steam. If only it tasted as good as it smelled, but this machine had come from a Union ship. I'd been meaning to replace the damned thing for the past few days, but between all the fighting and running, there had been no good opportunities.

Besides, *Titan* had its own food dispensers, and the cafeteria seemed to do a decent job at producing artificial coffee. I'd gotten used to it, putting off replacing my own machine. I wanted to slap myself for being so lazy.

All in good time, I thought, staring at the swirling drink in my hand. *First, we investigate this transmission, then we find a way out of the system and get a new coffee maker.*

"Jace, what are you doing?" asked Abigail, who was apparently watching me as I stood there.

I scoffed at the question. "Making coffee. What's it look like?"

"It looks like you're wasting time," she told me.

"Only a fool thinks caffeine is a waste," I said, turning my back to her.

At that moment, Freddie came walking into the lounge from the direction of the engine room. "Is someone making coffee?" he asked.

"Have a cup," I said, stepping away from the machine. "I've got mine already."

His eyes lit up. "Don't mind if I do!"

Dressler was right behind him. I eyed her as she quietly followed, saying nothing. She was still technically my prisoner…or was she a hostage? Or a guest? I couldn't keep track of the terminology.

Either way, she was here, and I'd have to figure out what to do with her soon. "Doc," I said, giving her a nod.

"Renegade," she returned, less hostile than I expected. "Can you tell me why there's a snowstorm outside the ship instead of dark space?"

"Oh, that," I said, taking a sip of coffee. It tasted terrible, but I pretended not to notice. "We received a transmission and decided to investigate."

"What about your friends? Shouldn't we be waiting for them to come find us?" asked Dressler.

"You want me to sit and wait out there with my hands in my pocket?" I asked. "Is that how you normally handle your problems?"

She glared at me. "I didn't say you should do *nothing*, but running down to a planet without a plan of action doesn't seem like the best use of our time. We should be focused on repairing the slip drive."

"Which is exactly what I want you to do," I answered. "Well, you and Fred. Someone needs to supervise the job."

"Are you concerned I might try to sabotage the ship?"

she asked, crossing her arms. "Maybe send a distress call to the Union, is that it?"

I paused. "I didn't think about that before, but now I'm starting to wonder."

"She won't do that," said Freddie.

"How the hell would you know?" I asked.

Freddie hesitated to answer, looking at the doctor for help.

"I wouldn't do that, because it would put us *all* in danger," said Dressler.

"You're right about that," said Abigail.

Freddie nodded. "*Exactly*. If she called the Union, they'd open fire on this ship, even if she's onboard."

"Unlike you, Captain Hughes, I value my life," said Dressler. She turned around and strode toward the engine room. When she got to the door, she glanced back over her shoulder. "Are you coming, Mr. Tabernacle?"

Freddie perked up at the sound of his last name. "Oh, right," he said, following after her.

I watched them leave together, staying quiet until they were out of earshot. "What do you think?" I asked, turning to Abigail.

"About what?"

"The doc," I said. "You think we should trust her?"

"We shouldn't trust anyone, but I don't think she'll do anything to risk her own life. She's not a soldier or a spy."

I nodded. "Siggy, continue to monitor repairs and let me know when the engines are back online."

"Yes, sir," said Sigmond, speaking directly into my earpiece.

"Once this storm lets up, we're heading out," I said, looking at Abigail and taking another sip of my coffee. This time, I openly cringed at the bitter taste.

Abby reached out and took the cup from my hand, taking a drink of it for herself. "I'll be ready."

2

THE STORM NEVER ACTUALLY DIED. It simply slowed to a steady crawl. Snow fell and would continue to do so for the next few days, according to Sigmond's scans. It was the best I could hope for, because it meant we could finally leave the ship and look for the source of that transmission.

I sat in my quarters, putting on the thickest jacket I had, along with some stuffed leggings and a snow cap. These clothes were specially made for cold weather, with internal heating that would regularly adjust to my body temperature. Useful to have when you spend your time running from one planet to another. You never knew what kind of hazards you'd run into. Better to over-prepare than not at all.

I zipped up the coat right as I stepped out of my room.

"Are you ready?" asked Abigail, her voice coming from across the lounge.

I glanced up from my chest to see her standing there, wearing the outfit I'd given her—form-fitting material stretching from neck to toe. It was thinner than mine, so much that it gave me pause.

She must have noticed, because she immediately rolled her eyes. "I can't believe this is all you had," she finally said, walking up to me.

"It adjusts to your body type," I said, which was the truth. The outfit was adaptable and could be worn by almost anyone, male or female. It tightened in order to better regulate internal body heat, which was necessary for severe weather.

"Uh huh," she said, glancing out the window of the ship. The snow was falling at a gentle pace. "Are you ready to head out?"

"I am if you are," I said.

She tapped the pistol on her thigh. "Let's see what's out there."

We went to the cargo bay, opening the lift door, letting in a breeze of cold wind. Snow trickled down on the metal grate of the gate, melting instantly. "I hate the cold," I muttered, opening one of the lockers and taking a rifle.

"You do seem like a beach person," Abigail said.

"Have you ever met anyone who wasn't?" I asked. "Give me a drink and a warm beach over a blizzard of cold any day of the week."

We stepped onto the gate and into the white field, with each step leaving a large hole in the snow. I wondered how long it would take for the storm to cover up these prints. Probably not long, given the rate it was falling.

I tapped my ear and activated the comm. "Siggy, where are Dressler and Freddie?"

"In the engine room, sir," answered the A.I.

"Open a line," I said, waiting for the click. After a moment, I continued. "Fred, this is Hughes."

"Yes, sir! I hear you, loud and clear," said Freddie.

"We're heading out and I'm ordering a lockdown on the ship. No one can enter or leave without my authorization. You got that? Keep your ass planted until we get back."

"Right, I understand," he said.

"And watch Dressler. Don't leave her alone."

"I'll stay with her at all times," he said.

"You'll *what?*" asked Dressler, a slight echo in her voice. "Are you talking to your captain? Tell him I'm doing what he asked and to stop treating me like—"

I cut the comm. "Siggy, initiate lockdown, my authorization."

"Initializing," said Sigmond. "The *Renegade Star* is secure. Sending transmission origin point to your pad. Good luck and try not to die, sir."

"Thanks, Siggy," I said, taking a step forward in the snow. "You do the same."

THE SNOW WAS harsh and thick, slowing our walk more than I expected. Even with the heating pads beneath my clothes, I could barely stand the cold winds as they blew in from the east. After only ten minutes, my cheeks had already gone numb. I was ready to leave this place.

Abigail seemed fine. She was outpacing me, and I didn't much like it. Maybe it was the better insulation in the clothes she wore. Maybe she'd spent time in weather like this at some point. Whatever the case, she was making me look bad, and gods knew I couldn't have that.

I quickened my pace and kept up with her. "Where to?" she asked as we reached the edge of the field.

Walls of rock surrounded the open valley. Scans had suggested there was a cave network inside the stone, and since the pad showed the signal coming from ahead and below, I knew we'd have to take the plunge. "We need to find a way inside," I said, looking over the scan.

"Inside what?" she asked.

I motioned at the wall.

"Are you serious?" she asked.

"I never joke about cave-diving," I answered.

The stone wall continued north and south, so I chose north and followed it. Abigail did the same, and together we began our search for a way inside.

After half an hour, we found a large enough gap to walk through. The split was narrow at first, but eventually opened up between two walls, forming an incline that descended further into the ground.

"Hold on, Jace," cautioned Abigail, touching my shoulder.

I paused and looked at her. "What is it?" I asked.

She motioned with her eyes to the ground, so I glanced at my feet. It was mostly covered in a thick layer of snow, but as the cave formed, the floor began to reveal itself. That was when I noticed what Abigail already had.

A set of stairs, finely cut and shaped into the stone, leading into the darkness. "Now we're talking," I finally said.

"We're on the right track," she told me, a slight smile on her face.

"I guess this means there really were people here," I said. "Or maybe there still are." I raised my hands, pretending to be spooky.

She rolled her eyes and kept walking, while I snickered at my own joke.

I ran a quick scan, which told us that we could take this path all the way down to the source of the transmission. It seemed a little too convenient, given my experience, but I wasn't about to argue with a machine.

Not that I was against that type of thing. Just ask Siggy.

We continued our descent, further into the cave. The stairs glimmered with frozen water, which told me to watch my step or I'd slip and break my neck if I wasn't careful.

As we reached the bottom and the passage opened, I

noticed the outside light began to fade. I tapped my pad and activated the flashlight, while Abby did the same with her wrist-pad. The corridor illuminated, revealing smoother stone walls and a flatter floor with etched lines.

Abby and I looked at each other. "I think we're on the right path," she told me.

I nodded. "The only question I have is—"

"Where did all the people go?" she asked, cutting me off.

I narrowed my eyes. "Watch it or I'll leave you down here."

She scoffed. "Nothing but talk," she said, smirking at me as she continued forward. "Do you think anyone's still alive down here?"

"If they are, they must be miserable," I said, shining my light around, trying to find anything that might give a hint as to what had happened here.

I guessed this must be the outer corridor, probably far from anything of value. Maybe we'd find some mummified tombs in here somewhere; maybe a hidden bunker full of ancient technology like the kind we came across on Epsilon, the planet with the original star map. Hell, maybe we were just wasting our time, but I couldn't shake the feeling that there was a secret here—a buried treasure beneath this blanket of snow and ice, lost to time and circumstance.

All I had to do was find it.

IT ONLY TOOK twenty minutes for the tunnel to open into a room, although it wasn't large or impressive. In fact, if it hadn't been for the doors and broken furniture, I would have thought we were still in a hallway.

I moved the light across the room, studying what I could of it. I had no idea what I was looking for, but you never know what you'll find if you just open your eyes.

Abby stood there for a moment, scanning the room and taking it all in. Most of the furniture appeared to be old and decrepit. There was a couch resting against the wall, large holes in its seat cushions. I briefly considered sitting on it, but figured it might crumble in the process.

The table, which had two missing legs, sat on its side next to the couch.

The opposite half of the room had a large, half-circle desk, its corners chipped and cracked. The seat behind it had withered away at some point, so much that only pieces of it remained.

"What was this place?" Abigail asked, her voice echoing.

I checked behind the desk but found nothing of value. Just dust and grime. "If I had to guess, I'd say this was the reception area."

"Reception?" she asked. "Like a doctor's office?"

I shrugged. "Who knows? It could've been anything."

She thought for a moment. "If this was a lobby, then —" She turned back to the way we came and pointed at the hall. "—that must be the entrance."

"This whole place reeks of government bureaucracy," I said.

Abby nodded, motioning to the closed door beside the desk. "Let's keep going."

I nestled my pad into my coat, grasping the door with my hands. "Ready when you are."

She did the same, planting her feet. "Okay," she muttered, taking a quick breath. "Pull!"

3

I⊤ ᴛᴏᴏᴋ some effort to pry the door open. We worked at it for nearly twenty minutes, and for a moment, I wasn't sure we'd ever get it cracked. Once we did, though, the rest was easy. The metal slid open, grinding against the doorway and into the wall, filling the area with a horrible, echoing screech.

"If anyone's here, they probably heard that," I said, stepping into the next hall.

"Do you really think there are still people living here?" asked Abigail.

"Who knows?" I asked. "But I wouldn't bet against it. Humans can survive anywhere. We're like rats."

"Rats can't survive anything," corrected Abigail.

I rolled my eyes. "Fine. Bacteria. Bugs. Whatever. You ever heard of Tolsados?"

"No," she said as we continued walking.

We came to a fallen beam in the middle of the hall. I took my time stepping over it, making sure I didn't cut my clothes and accidentally break the heating pads. "It was a colony in the Deadlands, probably a century ago. Nice planet, from what I saw in the pictures, but that was before the bombs."

"Someone dropped a bomb?" Abby asked, making her way across the beam.

I waited on the other side, offering my hand to help her. She took it, finally stepping clear of the debris. "Yeah, but it was more like a dozen of them. Nasty stuff. They wiped three hundred thousand people off the planet."

"That's awful," she said.

"That's war," I said, shaking my head. "Later on, a group of scrappers went down to the planet, looking to scavenge whatever they could find. One of them went off on his own and ended up finding a bunker full of survivors. Turns out, they'd been down there for nine years, terrified to go outside."

"Because of the radiation?" she asked.

I shook my head. "They used non-ionized clean bombs on the colony, so long-term radiation wasn't a problem. It was fear that kept them there. These people thought they'd get nuked again, so they decided to never leave. They had generators, a bio-garden, rations, running water. They'd *planned* for this scenario. By the time the scrappers found them, they'd already started having kids. Hell, they even had their own mini-government."

"That's crazy," said Abby.

"No argument here," I said, smirking. "All I'm saying is you can never count people out. Even when the world has gone to total shit, we'll find a way to keep going. We're stubborn like that."

We entered another room, this one with a taller ceiling and more intricate carvings in the walls. There were multiple workstations, which suggested we were closer to the heart of this place. I tried touching one of the computers, pressing different buttons and hoping for something to happen. I got nothing, as expected. No doubt, the power here had long since died, so getting any of this to work would be nearly impossible.

There was another doorway on the right-hand side of the room, seemingly torn from its place. It took me a moment, but I found it lying on the floor nearby, its metal bent and cracked. "Huh," I muttered, crouching over the door. "How do you figure this happened?"

"Earthquake?" asked Abigail. "This place looks like it's barely holding together."

I got to my feet, keeping my eyes on the fallen door. Abby was right about the facility. It looked like it was ready to cave in on itself, but that didn't explain the markings here. This looked like it had been beaten open. Had there been someone inside at some point? Trapped, maybe?

"Over here," said Abigail, walking to the edge of the

room. There was a wall with broken glass. "Looks like the window's shattered. Shine a light down there."

"Where?" I asked, walking closer to the opening and amplifying my pad's light. The area around me illuminated even more than it already had. I changed the option on the screen to narrow the light, allowing me to focus it to see further away.

I aimed the pad through the window, revealing a long drop into a larger warehouse. Containers littered the floor, varying in size and shape, suggesting this was a storage department. Maybe there was something valuable down here, after all.

"Want to check it out?" I asked, turning to Abigail. To my surprise, she was already out the door, looking down from the platform, into the warehouse. "I'll take that as a yes."

I swept the room again with my light, adjusting it to see a little more of the area at once. I didn't much care for this place. The smell of death was everywhere, and despite the lack of bodies, I knew something had happened here. Something awful.

"Are you coming?" asked Abigail. She had already tied a rope to the platform, fastening the other end to her waist, ready to climb the nearby ladder.

"After you," I said, watching her descend into the lower deck. I was right behind her, taking my time on the rickety ladder. Every step felt less secure than the last, leaving me to wonder if it was about to collapse from my weight. It didn't, and I successfully landed on the floor in due time.

Abigail walked several meters into the warehouse, shining her wrist-pad's light on the different crates, moving on from one to the next.

I approached one of the crates and felt around the upper edge for a lid. Digging my fingers into the crease, I managed to lift the cover enough to push it away and look inside.

"Hey, are you sure you should be doing that?" asked Abigail.

"How else are we supposed to investigate anything?" I asked, turning my light so I could see inside the box.

There was a stack of neatly laid cloth, folded and hardly worn. I was surprised to see how well preserved they were, although that could have been a result of the crate. Was it built for long-term storage? I'd heard certain containers, so long as they remained unexposed, might keep materials fresh and clean for several lifetimes, although I couldn't imagine why you would ever need such a thing.

Then again, now that I thought about it, Athena had mentioned that the Eternals from Earth could live much longer than the rest of us. Maybe all of this was meant for them.

Abigail opened another crate, prying the lid free of the body and checking inside. "Looks like clothes in this one," she said, lifting out an outfit, which was blue and resembled a kind of jumpsuit. She tossed it to me and I caught it, instantly noticing the patch on the shoulder—a series of letters identical to those found on *Titan*.

Using my pad, I snapped a picture of the patch. Sigmond might be able to translate the writing once we returned to the ship.

I checked my map, letting Abigail continue with whatever she was doing, and noticed we still had some distance to go before we reached the source of the transmission. The map also appeared to have filled out with the areas we'd explored already. So long as I had the feature on, the device would continue to scan, using line-of-sight to catalogue our progress.

"Jace, look at this," called Abigail from across the room.

I glanced up to see her squatting on the floor, examining a pile of fallen rubble. "What is it?"

I shined my light on the ground until I neared the wall. There was a gaping hole, twice the size of a standard door. Rocks and debris littered the area near our feet.

"This place is a wreck," said Abigail, finally standing. She glanced at the hole in the wall. "It looks like it goes on for a while."

I focused my light source, extending the range, and aimed it down the tunnel. She was right. I couldn't even see the end. "We need to go lower," I said. "Are there any other doors around here? Maybe some stairs?"

"Not that I can see," she said.

I checked the pad again. The source of the transmission

was ahead of us, several meters below our position. This tunnel seemed like it might lead us to where we needed to go, but how could that be? It couldn't have been built intentionally.

"Should we check it out?" asked Abigail.

I hesitated to answer, looking around the rest of the warehouse, hoping to find another way down. Maybe Abigail had missed something. Maybe there was a staircase somewhere.

No, we'd searched around and found nothing. I could see all the exits from here There was nothing else, no other path but forward. Somehow, this gaping hole in the wall was the only path we could take.

I stepped closer to the opening, leaning into it. "Guess we're going down," I finally said, looking at Abigail.

She nodded. "After you."

4

THE CAVE FLOOR was rockier than I expected, and I lost my footing more than once. The further we went, the more the air began to change, growing colder and forcing me to increase the heat in my suit.

I thought I noticed a smell too, although I wasn't sure at first. It was on the tip of my nose, and I wagered it was just my imagination, but the more we walked, the stronger the scent became. It was foul and rotten, like the trash you forget to take out before a long trip, only to find it stinking up the apartment a week later.

But despite the stench, I couldn't find the source. Maybe there was a dead animal nearby, hidden in the ice walls of this cavern. Who could really say?

The tunnel was long and winding, going further than I thought it would, taking us deeper and deeper into the ground. We walked slowly for half an hour before we found anything besides the jagged stone and ice that made up most of the corridor, but when we did, I had to stop and examine it.

It was a crate, the same kind we'd found in the warehouse, its lid ripped from its body and half sunk in the dirt, all its contents missing. Marks ran along the metal surface of the object—scratches, maybe—giving both of us pause as we stared down at it. "Jace," muttered Abigail, blinking at the box.

"I know," I said, bringing my voice to a whisper. "There's something else down here."

"It has to be some kind of animal," she said. "What do we do?"

I pulled out my rifle, checking the magazine and the safety. "We deal with it."

She nodded, unholstering her pistol.

Without another word, we continued through the tunnel to whatever was waiting for us up ahead.

———

THE SMELL HAD FINALLY GROWN SO strong that I had to cover my nose with my sleeve.

We neared a corner, descending further into the cave until the corridor opened into a larger cavern. The hard stone of the previous tunnel was gone, I realized, replaced with softer dirt and fresh ice.

Abigail spotted a pile of trash nearby—an assortment of broken things, such as metal wires and bars, shredded clothes, and…something else.

I leaned in closer, crouching beside the pile, trying to get a better look at it. With the light from my pad and using the barrel of my rifle, I moved the different pieces of trash around so I could better see. It took me a moment to realize what I was looking at—chalk-white sticks with etches in them. These were bones, I decided. The only question was, who or what did they belong to?

I showed them to Abigail, who didn't flinch or turn away. She only seemed to study them, waiting a few seconds before she gave me a response. "So we know it's a carnivore," she said, almost analytically.

I had to admit, I wasn't expecting that. "Do you think these are human remains?"

"Why would they be?" she asked. "There's no way anyone still lives here."

I motioned at the pile. "This could be from a grave somewhere."

She paused. "Now that you mention it, we haven't seen any skeletons yet."

She was right about that. Everything we'd seen up until now had been totally empty.

"Even if they are," she continued, "at least they were already dead. If these animals are going after corpses, they could just be scavengers. We might have already scared them away, just by being here."

"Sure," I muttered, staring at the bones at my feet.

"What? You don't agree?"

I wanted to, more than she probably knew. "I don't know." I turned and shined the light on the rest of the cavern, spotting more piles a few meters from our position. I walked closer to one of them and bent down. Sure enough, there were more bones here, similarly placed. "Whatever did this, it wasn't small. Those claw marks we saw on the box, back in the hall...they were huge. Same goes for the door we found in the warehouse. That kind of mark means there was muscle behind those claws."

"You're talking like you want to leave," she said.

I paused at the suggestion. I hadn't considered going back yet. Did I sound like I was afraid? "No, we're not giving up on this job. So long as we're armed, we'll be fine." I motioned at the pistol in her hand. "You watch my back. I'll watch yours."

She nodded. "You got it."

I glanced back at the pile in front of me. There was something else about these things, a feeling I couldn't shake. Animals generally didn't organize things in such methodical ways, not like this. The piles seemed to serve no purpose, unless I was missing it. They didn't look like a nest or anything useful that the creature might need later. They were more like little markers, signifying something.

The more I thought about it, the more I wondered. Were these piles meant to represent each kill? Or were they graves, built to remember the dead?

Either way, it meant there was an intelligence here, and it seemed eager to surround itself with death.

WE FOUND MORE piles as we continued through the tunnels, heading closer to the source of the signal. After a while, I stopped noticing them.

Part of me wondered if the animals had migrated someplace else or simply died off. Probably not, since the smell was so pungent that I could hardly stand to move my arm from my nose.

One of the tunnels brought us to another opening similar to the first, which led into a lower section of the facility. As we stepped through the gap in the wall, I quickly discovered how different this place was from the first.

Glowing lights illuminated throughout this new area, hinting at some kind of power. My focused light showed several consoles and dusty computer systems, blinking a rainbow of different-colored lights. I fought the urge to run up to them, and instead gripped my rifle tighter.

"The power source must still be partially active," said Abigail, gawking at the sight before us. "Do you know what this means?"

"I think you just told me," I muttered.

"There could be something salvageable. Maybe something we can use for the engine," she suggested.

I doubted that. Ship design was constantly changing,

and this place was old as hell. There was little to no chance we'd find anything compatible with the *Renegade Star*'s slip drive.

Still, she had a point. If this place had power, that might mean a working system with data logs. We might be able to learn what happened to these people and where they went. If nothing else, we had a few hundred crates with preserved cargo sitting in the upper warehouse, waiting to be salvaged.

I waved Abigail over and pointed to one of the terminals. "Think you can figure this out?"

"I'm not Dressler, but I'll try," she said, walking to the console.

"Yeah, I should've brought her instead," I joked.

She raised her brow but didn't look at me. "Let's see what we have here."

I watched Abigail as she tapped the console, then proceeded to pace around the room. The rear led into another corridor, its door sitting open but not broken. If any of those animals had come in here, they hadn't done much damage to the facility, and there were no signs of the bone piles, from what I could see. Who knew what lay ahead, though. We had to be ready for anything.

"It's no good," Abigail finally said, turning back to me. "The computer reacts, but most of the language is different. We need a translator."

I tapped my ear. "Siggy, you hear me?" I asked, waiting

for a response. Nothing came. "Siggy? This is Jace. You there?"

"We must be too far underground," suggested Abigail.

I lowered my hand and sighed. "This is going to be tough if I can't get Siggy on the line. We might have to bring a repeater system with us to amplify the signal."

She smirked. "Careful, Jace. You almost sound like you know what you're doing."

There was a sudden bang, like metal hitting metal, coming from the cave we had just arrived from.

Abigail and I reached for our guns instinctively, aiming at the large opening across the room from our position.

We waited, breathing quick, sharp breaths, a sudden burst of adrenaline coursing through our veins. The silence in the room was suddenly so thick and claustrophobic.

And the pounding in the cave was growing louder.

I squeezed the grip of my rifle, letting out a slow breath that filled the freezing cold air in front of me like steam.

That was when we saw it.

A hulking, monstrous thing, hunching forward and dragging its hands, but still nearly as tall as the cave itself. Its body was covered in a thick coat of white fur, so much that you couldn't see its eyes.

The animal reached up, gripping the edge of the door-way. When it did, I finally noticed the shape of its hands, each consisting of three large claws. I imagined one of those would easily be enough to impale me, should I be so unlucky.

The creature paused, taking a moment to look into the room. It tilted its head but didn't seem to notice us. I wondered if it saw the light from my pad and the console.

But the creature didn't seem to care. Instead, it stared out into the room, at nothing in particular, strangely still and quiet.

The light of the pad shined on its face, but I still couldn't see its eyes. Where was it looking? What did it see?

The animal took another whiff of air, then stepped forward and into the room.

Abigail swallowed, and in the silence of this place, it echoed louder than it should have.

Fuck, I thought.

The beast's head perked up, pausing as its ears reached their peak.

I turned, looking over my shoulder at the hall behind us. If we moved quickly, we could get there and bottleneck this animal inside. That would make for an easy target, so long as we kept our distance. Better than a room as large as this one.

Abigail noticed me. I flicked my eyes back and forth to the door, letting her know the plan. She seemed to grasp it, giving me a slight nod. Good, we were in agreement.

The creature took another step towards us, still keeping its ears up. By this point, I was beginning to understand how it worked. We were only a few meters away, so I wagered it couldn't see us. Not the same way we could see it.

But I wasn't a zoologist, and I didn't have time to sit here and analyze whatever the hell this thing was. All I knew was that I had to move, shoot, and kill this bastard dead.

Abigail stared at me, holding her breath, and waited.

I moved my eyes back to the monster, letting them linger on him for a few seconds, making sure he wasn't moving, and then finally returned to Abigail. With a quick nod, I gave her the signal to move, and suddenly, she did.

I grabbed the pad on the counter and we bolted for the hall behind us.

The moment we moved, I heard the monster grunt, letting out a wheeze that resembled a clogged engine, followed by a snarling yelp. It slammed its two arms against the ground, pounding them in rage, and took off in our direction, sending echoing booms throughout the facility with every terrible step.

We filed through the corridor entrance and into the rear. I turned my whole body back around, swinging my barrel and taking aim at the opening. Abigail did the same, and the second the white-furred creature came into view, we unloaded on it.

The hall was narrow, and the animal had a hard time fitting in. It tried to squeeze through, swiping its claws at us, but remained out of range. The doorway cracked, breaking as the pressure built. It wouldn't hold for long.

I kept firing. The creature seemed to absorb the bullets,

so full of rage and fury, barely moving. I stepped back, one foot at a time, keeping my distance.

The animal roared, slamming its shoulders into the doorway.

"Enough of this!" barked Abigail. She ran up closer to it, just out of range from its claws.

In one fluid motion, Abby brought her weapon up to the animal's mouth. The creature snapped at her, but not before she fired one last shot into its mouth.

Brains splattered out the back of its skull, spraying its white coat with green blood as its face dropped lifelessly to the floor.

The floor rumbled as the animal collapsed before us.

We watched it for a moment, neither of us saying a word. Maybe we were being cautious, considering this animal had just taken a magazine's worth of bullets and still managed to get itself halfway through the hall. "I think we got it," Abigail finally muttered.

I edged my way closer to the monster, keeping my rifle aimed on him, ready to shoot if, somehow, he'd survived a direct shot to the face. It wouldn't be the first time an animal's brain was in a place other than its head, rare as it might be.

With my barrel, I nudged its head, lifting its chin to see its lifeless face. For the first time, I managed to get a decent view of its eyes…or the lack thereof, since it didn't seem to have any. Instead, there were only black spots where the eyes should be, nestled between white fur.

I let the head fall and hit the floor again. "I think we're good," I said.

"Do you think these things killed the colonists?" asked Abigail.

"Maybe," I said, looking up at the collapsed wall where the door had been. How were we going to get out of here?

I stepped over the creature's leg and felt the debris beneath my foot, but didn't put much pressure on it. Moving it might pull down the rest of the ceiling, and I couldn't have that.

I glanced at Abigail's wrist-pad, which was still shining bright enough to fill the corridor. "Can you take pictures with that thing?" I asked.

"Huh? What for?" she asked.

"The signal down here is awful, but if we can work our way a few levels higher, we might be able to get a message to Siggy," I said, walking back over to her. "Probably not a direct call, but images might send easier."

"Okay," she said. "But what do you want pictures of?"

I looked at the dead monster at my feet. "What do you think?"

She scoffed. "Right. Let me just pull up the camera app."

I got out of the way, taking a step behind her, and tried to make out the next room. It looked similar to the last, filled with consoles and machines, many of them blinking a variety of colored lights. I still couldn't believe this place had power.

Abigail walked closer to the animal and began snapping pictures.

"Make sure you get the face," I said.

She did, snapping multiple angles. We'd have to attach a written message to the images. Something like, *Dear idiots, we found some deadly animals. Don't leave the ship.* That would probably do the trick.

Abigail wiped some sweat from her forehead, backing up toward me. "I think that's enough," she said, lowering her arm. She swallowed, then took out a small container of water and sipped it, gasping as she put it away. "What now? Where are we going?"

I stared into the darkness before us. "Deeper," I muttered, finally stepping out of the hall and into the next room. "We just keep going deeper."

5

I HADN'T REALIZED it at first, but we were still following the path to the source of the transmission. Despite the tunnel we took and the fight in that last room, our overall course never changed. Unless we discovered a way out of here soon, we were still going to accomplish our mission, simply by following the path ahead of us.

That was fine with me. We didn't come all the way down here just to wind up with nothing. Of course, at this point, I was more concerned with escaping these godsforsaken catacombs than finding whatever black box was sending out that signal.

Best case scenario had me running across a staircase to the surface, going up to catch my breath, and finally coming back with some bigger and badder guns at my side.

But I knew the odds of that happening were slim. Whatever was ahead, we'd have to deal with what we had and hope for the best.

Strangely, Abigail soon spotted a staircase, although it only went down. I nearly laughed when I saw it. *Keep it up*, I thought, pretending that this place could hear me. I'm loving the irony.

A minute later, we passed from one hall to the next, only to discover a side room with multiple devices. Pods, actually, if I remembered right.

Several of them appeared to be active, if the lights were to be believed. As I neared them, I became even more certain, since the bed inside matched the ones from *Titan* almost exactly. "Do you recognize these?" asked Abigail, who must have noticed my slack-jawed expression.

"Yeah," I said, peering inside before touching one of the pods' cases. "I've seen them before…back on the moon."

"*Titan?*" she asked. "They don't look like the ones from the medical bay. Are you certain?"

I nodded. "There were more on another deck. Not medical pods."

"What were they for?" she asked.

"Long-term stasis, best that I could tell," I said. "Athena told me that was where Lex was born."

Abigail stopped. "What?"

I turned around and looked at her. "I've been meaning

to tell you, but it turns out Lex was born on *Titan* about two thousand years ago. Her parents were killed in some sort of terrorist attack, and then the scientists stuck her in a cryo-pod, just like these. When everyone left the ship and took off, no one bothered to wake her up."

Athena's mouth dropped. "And you kept this all to yourself?!"

"I've been a little busy," I said.

She scoffed. "When did you even learn about this in the first place? Was it before the last battle with Brigham?"

I said nothing.

"It was, wasn't it!" she snapped.

I shrugged. "Hard to remember."

She let out a groan of frustration. "I swear to gods. Was there anything else? Any other revelations you forgot to share?"

I thought for a moment while we continued walking. "Now that you mention it, Athena also told me the folks who left Earth were just a bunch of laborers that rebelled against some rich immortals."

She stopped again. "Wait...what?"

AFTER RELAYING everything I could remember, Abigail was uncharacteristically quiet for some time. I figured she just needed to process everything I'd just told her. After all, it's not every day you learn the true history of your ancestors. I tossed in the words Transient and Eternal, taking a second to explain them as best I could, and while I couldn't give her the same level of detail Athena had, I liked to think I did a decent job of it.

"Thank you for telling me, Jace," Abigail said after a while. The tone in her voice had turned gentle, like all the frustration had drained, replaced by contemplation. "I'll have to speak with Dr. Hitchens about all this."

"I meant to do that at some point," I said.

She only nodded, staring at the floor in front of her as we walked.

I realized all of this must be a lot for her to take in. It certainly had been for me. If she needed time to think, I'd give it to her.

We walked through the abandoned building for gods-knew-how-long. Our path kept us moving forward, on towards the beacon. It was just ahead now, not much further. Twenty meters, maybe, according to my pad.

Abigail was still quiet, her eyes lost in thought.

I decided she'd had long enough to wallow. I needed my partner ready for whatever lay ahead of us. "Abigail," I whispered, pausing to check the chamber of my rifle, ensuring I was set. I gripped the gun, aiming straight ahead of us at the open door, not far from the beacon. "Are you ready?"

She paused and looked at me. I stared back at her, waiting for her to realize what I was saying.

A second later, she blinked, finally understanding. She took the pistol and cocked it, giving me a short nod. Good. She was back. No more thinking. No more internal debating. That was the sort of thing that got you killed.

"Watch my back," I said as we stepped forward.

The light on my gun shined through the opening. As I entered it, I found a room covered in ice and stalagmites, wrought with age and decay, frozen over. Computer systems lined the walls, some of them still powered on. One of them stood out, its wide, fat body standing taller and larger than any other, with a cracked screen on the front of it.

I eased closer to it, trying to get a better look.

I retrieved my pad to verify that this was the right spot.

"Is this it?" asked Abigail.

"Looks like it," I muttered, putting the pad away and wiping some frost from the nearby machine. The screen was nearly frozen over, its contents difficult to read.

Make that impossible, I thought, realizing that whatever I found would almost certainly be in a foreign language.

Abigail eased herself closer. "Let me see," she said, nudging into me. She tapped the screen, causing it to change. "Hey, look at that."

"Be careful," I said. "You don't know what you're doing."

Several lines of text appeared, each in a different color. It had to be a menu, an interface to guide users, not unlike the one on my ship.

Abigail tapped what seemed like a random menu item,

bringing up another screen. It flickered rapidly for a moment before reverting to the previous menu. "Must be buggy," I said.

"After sitting here for so long in—" She glanced around the cavern. "—these *conditions*, I'm surprised it still works at all." She tapped the screen, trying another menu option.

Like the previous one, when Abigail clicked the new option, the screen bugged out and returned to the first interface.

She cursed under her breath. "Hold on. I'll try again."

I watched her select multiple options, each without success. It might take her days to figure this out, but even then, we still wouldn't be able to read the text.

"Relax," I told her, placing a hand on her shoulder. "Let's head topside and see if we can get those repeaters set up. Might be better to have Dressler and Siggy doing this. This isn't our area of expertise. What do you—"

A sudden thud shook the floor under my feet. I felt the vibration rattle up my legs. I turned around, gun pointed and ready.

Abigail raised her weapon, covering one of the other doorways. There were three connections to this room, one on every wall, except the side with the terminal. If we were attacked, it could come from any direction.

I waited, listening intently. I could almost feel my heart pounding inside my chest, and every breath I took echoed in this place, louder than I could have expected.

That was when I heard the second thud, so much louder than the first.

I got a sense of the direction. Straight ahead of me—to the right of the computer. Abby swung around to face it too, each of us backing up so we had plenty of time to shoot.

THOM.

THOM.

The pounding had grown faster, louder than before. Those were footsteps, but slow and heavy. Another one of those monsters.

THOM.

THOM.

THOM.

My gun's light shined against the ice, far ahead and beyond the doorway, until it faded into darkness. There, in the shadow of the frozen hall, I spotted a reflection, glistening as it moved like waving grass.

The monster stepped forward, revealing its long, white hair, thick and full with the light of my pad. The dark spots where its eyes should be stared blankly in my direction, and its ears perked up, the same as the last.

I noticed this one was smaller, thinner. I guessed it was still young. Maybe we'd killed its parent, or perhaps it was only the runt of a larger group.

Either way, things were about to get messy.

THOM.

My eyes widened. The animal had been standing totally motionless. Where had that sound come from?

THOM.

THOM.

I slowly turned to my right, following the new noise. It was another hallway, different from where the first creature stood.

THOM.

THOM.

THOM.

A shadow crept against the wall on the other side of the doorway, the monstrous beast dragging both its massive arms.

With my left hand, I slowly nudged Abigail, tipping my head toward the only remaining path, the opening behind us.

She resisted for only a split-second, dropping her natural defenses when she understood what I was telling her, and reached down and took my hand, giving it a gentle squeeze.

Good, I thought. *She understands. Okay.*

THOM.

Another footstep and I finally saw the claws, slowly coming around the tunnel.

THOM.

The rest of the beast came into view, pausing when it reached the threshold of the room.

The first animal bent its head towards the second, then let out a loud bark.

The second tilted his head, flicking his ears, and then returned the noise with something similar. A deeper grunt.

The first stood tall, raising up its hands and pounding its chest, barking once more.

This was it. We had to go. Fight or flight. Run or die. "Move!" I snapped, leaping back and firing.

Bullets shot across the room as the two monsters yelped. The combined noise of gunfire and screaming hit my ears with so much intensity that I thought I might go deaf.

I ran backwards, nearly tripping on the ice. The two beasts lunged at me, their long arms coming so close, they nearly took my stomach from me.

I fled into the rear hall, firing blindly behind me, no concern for what I hit. Abigail was already at the back of the corridor, turned toward me with her gun extended. "Get down!" she shouted.

I slid beneath her, pivoting on the ice to face the animals. Abigail fired her pistol, shots hitting each of the creatures.

On my back, I fired my rifle between my legs, unloading the magazine.

The runt took several shots in the shoulder, neck, and chest before slowing. I got lucky, managing to tag him in the knee, splitting the animal's joint and forcing him to the floor. He slid, screaming, while the other and much larger of the two continued his pursuit.

"Run!" I shouted, getting to my feet.

Abby turned and fled alongside me, each of us heading down the long corridor.

We had no idea where we were going, no way to know what was up ahead. All we could do was run and try to get as many shots in on this thing as possible before it finally caught up.

Which wouldn't be long, I quickly realized, glancing over my shoulder.

The animal ran with more speed than I had expected, pounding the ice with its massive legs and clawed hands. It was so loud, I could feel the movement in my chest.

Abby and I raced through the hall, the beast shortly behind. I raised my weapon and fired, letting out a few shots before I heard a click. "I'm out!" I shouted.

"Me too!" she replied.

We rounded a corner, and I slammed my shoulder into the ice wall, then pushed forward and continued sprinting.

"Tessa! Tessa!"

"What?!" I asked.

"I didn't say anything!" Abby answered.

"Tessa!" came the voice again. I looked ahead to see a figure, waiting at the end of the hall, waving both arms. "Tessa modune! Tessa!"

"Who the hell?" I asked, but there was no time to answer. We were already arriving.

The stranger, dressed in an assortment of pelts and furs, and wearing a large mask, waited for us to leave the hallway before stepping in front of the oncoming animal. In a fluid motion, she swept her hand beneath her garment and retrieved a sort of stick—no, it was a rifle, I instantly realized. "Sachala!" she shouted at the beast. "*Sachala rockheme!*"

The end of the barrel glowed blue and white before releasing an explosive blast on the monster, just before it reached us. The light pierced the creature's shoulder, knocking it back a few steps.

The monster staggered, dragging its claws on the floor. It shook its head, spitting into the air, and then leaned forward and roared.

I flinched at the sound, it was so loud.

The animal raised its claws and pounded the area around it. A show of force.

The woman kept the gun aimed on the creature, ready to fire a second time, should she need to.

The animal wailed and raged at us, foaming at the mouth.

Right when I thought the stranger might fire her blue stick again, the animal jerked its claws above its head, scratching the ceiling and the ice, cracking it, and slamming its fists down.

The ceiling must have already been weak, because that was all it took to bring it crumbling down. Ice and metal collapsed on the animal, burying it in what seemed an endless pile of ruined foundation.

Dust scattered in every direction, hitting me like a

storm. I reached for Abigail, who was right beside me, and brought her to the floor just in time for the blast to hit us.

We tumbled, the wind sweeping across our backs, the avalanche still falling as it boomed with thunderous destruction. I expected the entire facility to come falling down at any moment, sending us to join all the other corpses that had once called this place their home.

6

I OPENED my eyes in Abigail's hair, snow falling all around us from the cave-in. She looked up at me, blinking and confused.

I moved back, and as I did, more dirt slid off my back. I offered my hand to her, which she took, and I pulled her up. We swiped our clothes, but the snow seemed never-ending.

"Gods," muttered Abby, wiping her forehead. "Let's not do that again, please."

We both looked at the stranger, who was staring at the fallen monster in the outer hall. She hadn't moved, despite everything that had just happened.

"Hey," I said, trying to get her attention. "Who are you?"

The woman turned to me, the skull-mask covering her

face. Now that I was close enough, I could see the shape of the skull more clearly. It seemed to be from one of those animals, with odd markings etched along the bone. They were familiar, like the kind I'd seen on *Titan*, but more specifically the tattoos Lex and I both shared.

"Are you listening to me?" I took a step closer to the woman. "I asked who you are."

"Badalaka," said the woman. "Dusaka, kei la."

I looked at Abigail. "Did you catch that?"

The nun shook her head. "I've never heard that language before."

"Badalaka!" shouted the skull-faced woman.

"We don't understand," I responded.

The stranger took a step closer to me, stopping a few meters away. She raised her stick—the weapon she'd just attacked that animal with—and began to point it at me.

I instinctively went for my rifle, but felt Abigail's hand on my wrist. "Hold on," she told me. "Wait."

The other woman extended the stick toward my neck, pushing my collar away, revealing the beginning of my tattoo. "Koraka," she whispered.

"What?" I asked, peering down at the stick.

The stranger pulled the weapon back. "Fordo," she said, gripping her skull mask and pulling it away.

I was surprised at her appearance—pale skin and blue eyes, with tattoos going from above her ear down to her neck. What exactly was I looking at?

"Fordo ack bala," said the woman. She seemed to be

older, possibly in her late sixties, if the wrinkles around her eyes were any indication. Who could say what effects this world might have had on her health? Maybe she was only thirty-seven.

"Yeah, hello to you too," I answered.

The woman pointed behind us with her stick. "Soga," she said, and started walking, heading directly between the two of us.

We turned with her, watching as she walked calmly to the back of the room, near a sealed door. She leaned over and tapped a small screen on the wall, causing the door to slide open. "Soga," she said again, looking back at us.

Abigail, still with her pistol out, looked at me. "What do you think?"

"Doesn't matter," I said, thumbing at the collapsed hallway with the newly deceased monster. "There's nowhere else to go."

Abby hesitated but ultimately conceded. "If she tries anything—"

"We'll handle it," I finished, and together we followed after the stranger.

I watched the old woman open several doors, each with the same code.

2-0-1-1-9

I quickly memorized the sequence, because why the hell wouldn't I?

The raggedy hag brought us to a hall with glass walls on either side. The rooms here seemed to be made for meetings, with ancient tables at the center and what I guessed were broken chairs surrounding them, although it was difficult to tell with all the rubble and debris.

At the end of all this, the woman took us to another door, this one opening into a tall staircase. She pointed her blue stick into the air, saying something I decided must mean "Up" or "Go."

Either way, that was exactly what we did. She led us through seven flights, never slowing, despite her age. I decided that whatever happened next, I respected her. She'd killed an animal twice my size and still had the energy to climb all these steps. *Not bad, lady. Not bad.*

When we reached our destination floor, there was a sealed door, although it didn't look like the others. This one didn't slide between the wall when you entered a code. It was more traditional than that, attached directly to the side so it swung open. She banged on the metal with her stick three times. Twice in succession, then a short pause before the final tap.

The door creaked open, echoing in the stairwell.

A face appeared between the widening crack in the door, covered with another mask. This one was metallic, probably made with parts and scraps from around this facility. I wondered briefly why the old woman had used the bones of an animal instead of metal shards like this person, but dismissed the thought. I'd have plenty of time to think about things that didn't matter, once I was out of this place. For now, I had to keep my wits about me, should any of these people prove a danger.

The man with the metal mask looked at the old woman before glancing at me. "Chala," he said, and I could see his eyes go wide from behind his mask. "Chala do ray!"

The old woman nodded, pointing to her own mask. "Dusaka es graw, chala do ray."

The man slowly nodded, then opened the door the rest of the way. I spotted a few people on the other side, watching us from afar.

The old woman looked at me, pointing with her stick to the open door. "Tak."

"I guess this means we're invited to dinner," I said, stepping through the opening, passing the two masked individuals.

Abigail followed, staying close to me. "I just hope we're not part of the main course," she whispered.

THE OLD WOMAN and her friend took us through what I could only assume was the general gathering area. It looked like another warehouse-sized room with tall ceilings. No crates, though. If any had ever existed in this place, I guessed they had been relocated or destroyed some time ago.

There were dozens of people here, each of them actively engaged with something. I saw some distributing supplies to one another, while children played nearby. *Kids*, I thought as one of them passed by us, laughing with her friend. *Even in a place like this, people find the time to make more people.*

Our hosts led us to another door, where a second guard was standing by. He stepped aside immediately, no doubt conceding his authority to the old woman and her friend.

The door opened, and we followed, taking us to a small area shaped like a circle, mats along the floor. There was someone already there, a younger woman who, like everyone else in this place, had pale skin, white hair, and blue eyes.

"Edda," said the old woman, nodding at the younger one. "Dusaka es graw, din mohala kin ro."

The younger woman, who I had to assume was the leader here, stared up at us. More specifically, at me, and seemed to consider us for a long moment.

"Tucka del ka," said the young woman. She looked at her older associate. "Sadda."

The old woman nodded, motioning to the nearest mats as she proceeded to the other side to take her seat. She folded her legs and sat her stick beside her, fully removing her mask and staring at me.

I glanced at Abby, and she shrugged.

"This ought to be interesting," I said, taking the same position the two pale women had, but across the circle.

Abigail sat beside me, and together we waited for what I could only assume would be some kind of tribal ritual.

The guard stepped outside and closed the door behind him, leaving the four of us alone.

"Tosha," said the younger woman, not looking away from me.

The older woman reached behind her for a small box, opening the lid and retrieving something from inside. Some kind of object, which she quickly and carefully handed to the one in charge.

The younger woman unwrapped the cloth, revealing a small device. I was about to ask what it was when she went to touch it, causing her tattoos to glow, along with the device.

I looked at Abigail, whose eyes had widened. We both knew full well what kind of technology this was, and that made us more than concerned. If these people were using ancient machines from Earth, there'd be no telling what they were capable of, especially when it came to weapons.

The younger woman held out her hand, the device resting on her palm, glowing with a soft, blue light.

"Taloka," she said, looking at me.

I stared at her, not understanding.

"Taloka," she said again.

I looked at the old woman, who pointed to her mouth. "Taloka," she said, repeating the word.

"I don't know what you're saying," I answered.

"Maybe they want you to eat it," said Abigail, raising her brow at me.

She was only half-joking, since neither of us could make out what any of this meant. How were you supposed to cross a language barrier like this? Oh, sure, there were different dialects all across the known galaxy, but most people continued to use Common E, since it was the official language of the Union government, all trade organizations, and even the Sarkonian Empire.

I reached out for the device, but the woman pulled her hand away, shaking her head. "Taloka," she said, pointing to her mouth.

"I already told you, I don't know what that means," I said. "You people keep talking gibberish like we're supposed to understand."

"Maybe if we return to the ship, Sigmond can translate for us," said Abigail.

The woman let her hand out again, opening her palm. She pointed at her mouth. "Taloka."

I sighed. "This is getting us nowhere."

"Giving up already?" asked Abigail.

"I didn't say that," I responded.

"What's the plan, then?" she asked.

"We just gotta figure out how to tell them we need to get topside," I said. "That'll be a challenge all on its own."

"What do you suggest?" she asked. "Nonverbals?"

"Aren't you good at that sort of thing?" I asked.

"Should I be?" she asked.

I cocked my eye. "Isn't part of your job knowing how to analyze body language?"

"That doesn't mean I'm good at charades," she said. "Maybe you can try pointing *up* and telling them we need to—"

"You would like to return to the surface?" asked the woman, suddenly speaking the same language.

I stared at her, uncertain of what I'd just heard. "Uh, *what?*"

Abigail blinked. "Did she just—"

"Ah, so you understand," said the young woman. "Good."

"You speak…?" My mouth fell slightly agape as I tried to process what I was hearing. "You know Common?"

"What is Common?" she asked.

Abigail looked at me then back at the woman. "The language you're speaking right now, it's—"

"What you're hearing is a translation," said the woman. She turned the glowing orb in her fingers. "I do not know your language. The machine speaks for me, just as it does for you."

"That's a translator?" asked Abigail.

We both gawked at the device. Mobile translators weren't uncommon in the Union, but I'd never seen one like this. It had the same color as the rest of the old Earth tech, blue and beautiful. Judging by the way these people were dressed, they couldn't have the knowledge to build something like this on their own. Had they found it some-where in the ruins we'd explored on our way here?

"The machine is one of many," said the woman. "We have a great deal of technology and are scavenging more each day. The process is long and difficult, and time has not been kind to these caves."

"So you found it?" I asked. "Did you also salvage the staff that buried the animal in the tunnel?"

The young woman glanced at her older friend, giving her a slight nod.

The older woman leaned forward. "I built this staff myself," she said, a hint of pride in her voice. "I salvaged its core and weaved its parts. Only the strongest of us have done so."

"Okay, okay," I said, fanning my hand at her.

"And the monster you hit with it?" asked Abigail.

The younger woman answered this time. "We call them Boneclaws. They patrol the tunnels you were in as well as the abandoned areas."

"Abandoned?" asked the nun. "You mean the old facility we saw?"

"What kind of name is Boneclaw?" I asked, mostly to myself.

The woman ignored me. "This entire structure was built by our ancestors when they came to this world."

"Came to this world from where?" Abby asked.

"From Earth," she answered.

I sat up, my interest suddenly piqued. I couldn't give a

damn about the animals, the snowstorms, of half the other stuff I was hearing. My goal was the same now as it had been when I first heard that transmission—finding out what the hell this godsforsaken place had to do with Earth.

"What do you know about Earth?" I asked them.

The younger woman stared at me for a brief moment. "I could ask you the same, boy."

I didn't say anything.

She smirked at my silence. "My name is Karin Braid." She motioned to the older woman beside her. "This is my mother, Lucia. We are the leaders of this encampment. All three hundred souls."

Abby smiled. "I'm Abigail Pryar. This is Jace Hughes."

"It is so wonderful to meet you," said Karin, a genuine sense of joy in her voice.

"How many more are there, besides your group?" asked Abigail.

"There are no others," said Karin.

"Not even in other parts of the facility?" asked Abby.

The older woman, Lucia, shook her head. "The cold kills any who leave."

"There are only three hundred of you on the entire planet?" asked Abigail. "How is that possible? Shouldn't there be more by now?"

"By now?" echoed Karin.

"Do you know when your ancestors left Earth?" asked Abigail. "Do you know when they came here?"

Karin looked at her mother, who was happy to answer.

"The records say it was over two thousand years ago, but the colony continued to grow long after that. It wasn't until the Boneclaws and the storms that our numbers diminished."

I paused, turning the words over in my head. "Did you just say the Boneclaws *arrived*? What does that mean? Weren't they always here?"

She shook her head. "No, not if the record keeper is to be believed."

"The record keeper?" asked Abigail.

"Janus," said Karin. "He holds all the knowledge of our history."

"Most of it," corrected Lucia.

Karin nodded. "Yes, most. I apologize."

Her mother smiled at her approvingly. "You asked about Earth," she said, turning to me. "What we know is limited, but Janus tells us that it is where our ancestors came from."

"Another world, far away," said Karin.

"The histories say it is a land of plenty, full of life," said Lucia. "A better place than this."

"Better is subjective," I said.

"Perhaps," said Lucia. "But live long enough among us and tell me there is no world worse than this one."

I didn't argue. These people had terrible lives. They knew it. I knew it. There was no point in a debate. "You keep talking about worlds," I finally said. "What do you know about that?"

"We're not fools," said Karin. "We may live in the ground, but each of us has been educated and fully understands why and how we came to be here."

"We also know you're not from this planet," added Lucia.

"What was that?" asked Abigail.

"Our defense network is down, so we couldn't send a message, but we saw your ship when it entered orbit," said Karin. "You may think we're nothing but savages, but you're the first visitors we've ever had and we saw you coming, probably before you even knew about us."

Not only that, but they seemed to know a thing or two about Earth technology. No, these weren't savages at all. I'd known that when I first saw the old woman use her staff against that monster in the tunnel. "Fair enough," I finally said. "We flew down here because there was a signal coming from the facility here. It mentioned Earth, so we investigated."

Karin smiled. "Now is when you tell me what you know about Earth, Mr. Hughes."

"Not much," I said. "No one's been there in thousands of years." I decided to leave out the part about Athena, *Titan*, and Lex. Those three were in high demand right now. Better to keep things brief until we learned more about these people. For all I knew, they'd try to steal my ship and hunt down the rest of my crew. Shit, we already had two empires after us.

"That's too bad," said Karin. "I was hoping you could

tell us something more, perhaps about what happened to it."

I shrugged. "Beats me, lady. I've heard it's out there, same as you, but I've never seen squat. Why do you think I came all the way down here? You've got a transmission talking about a planet no one has seen in ages. Of course I'm going to check it out."

Abigail didn't look at me. She only gave the two women a short nod.

Good, I thought. *She gets it.*

"If you've never seen images of Earth, you should," said Karin. "They are quite beautiful. Lush, green hills, wide open plains, and gorgeous blue skies."

"You've seen holos of it?" I asked.

"Janus shows them. If you'd like, I can arrange a meeting," said Karin. "He's with his students now, but we can take you there now."

"You'd do that?" asked Abigail. "Even though you don't know us?"

Karin smiled. "You're the first visitors we've ever had, remember? It would be a shame if we didn't treat you well. That's how it works with guests, right?"

"Right," said Abigail, returning the young woman's smile.

"Besides, if you try anything, we'll kill you," said Lucia, reaching for her staff. She tapped it with her palm, like it was a pet, and looked right at me. "Is that understood?"

7

KARIN LED us out of the round room and into another corridor, adjacent to the larger room we'd come from. After we passed by a few dozen more areas, I began to think this facility might go on forever. How big could it even be?

A few minutes into our walk, Karin's mother said something in their native language and broke off into another room. She seemed to have an urgency about her, but I didn't bother questioning it. Given the state of this place, I had to imagine there were a hundred grade-A disasters happening at any given moment.

"Hey, Abby," I said, stepping closer to her as we followed behind Karin.

"What?" she asked. "Don't tell me you have to use the bathroom or something."

"What do you think happened here?" I asked, ignoring her last remark.

"Probably the storms and the animals," she said. "Isn't that what they told us?"

"I can't see how that could wipe out an entire colony," I said.

"Maybe you can ask this Janus person," said Abby.

"Whoever he is," I muttered.

We continued past a group of men, each of them with tools and pieces of technology in their hands. I only caught a brief glimpse, but I could tell they were using salvaged scraps to fashion something new. Whether they were weapons or not, I couldn't know, not without asking, and I planned to do plenty of that very soon. Whoever this Janus person was, I hoped he could shed some light on what exactly happened here and why these people weren't connected to the rest of the galaxy anymore.

Karin brought us to an open doorway, and I heard laughter echo from the other side. There were children, lively and happy, a surprising sound in a place so dreary. As we stepped through, I saw that this was a classroom, with students sitting cross-legged on the floor, watching the teacher as he spoke. A man with a full head of white hair, just like the others, but still not quite the same. When I looked at him, and he moved, I thought I could see a glimmer of light against his skin, like I was watching a holo.

I noticed the teacher was speaking another language to the kids, the same one we'd heard earlier. Before I could say

64

anything about it, Karin retrieved the translator and held it out in front of her. The device glowed with a soft blue, and suddenly, the language transformed into something familiar.

"Fusion cores can be found across all three facilities on this planet, despite their high value," said the teacher. "You will need to fully understand them if you wish to survive in the caves and defend the village. That includes retrieval, maintenance, and functionality. Remember, such objects are not common, so it will take some effort to locate them."

The students watched their teacher with wide-eyed interest, like he was giving them a great truth…the secrets to the universe.

Hell, maybe he was. How was I supposed to know?

The teacher looked up at us, his eyes lingering on me for a brief moment. I wondered what he thought, what all of them thought, when they looked at me and Abigail. We looked nothing like any of them. Neither of us had white hair or blue eyes or pale skin. We stuck out like a couple of sore thumbs in a place like this, the same way Lex stood out in the rest of the galaxy. Now that I thought about it, I wondered how she might feel to be here with me and the rest of these people. She'd spent so long in hiding before now. Would it be better for her if she'd been born in a place like this? Would she be happier, even if it meant monsters and snowstorms?

"Excuse me a moment, class," said the teacher. "It

seems I am needed. Please stay seated and speak amongst yourselves. I'll resume the lesson momentarily."

The children began to mumble, their voices growing louder as the teacher began to walk towards us. He looked at both Abigail and me, and then again at Karin, as he finally approached. "Ms. Braid," greeted the teacher.

"Janus," responded Karin.

"I see we have visitors," he said, glancing at me.

"You were right," she said. "You said they would come."

He nodded. "It was only a matter of time."

I raised my brow. "Why aren't you more surprised to see us?"

"I've seen a great many things," he said. "After two thousand years, very little surprises me."

"Two thousand years?" asked Abigail.

I noticed another glimmer along Janus's sleeve, a reflection of light from a source that wasn't there. I saw no windows in this place, no bright sources of light, only dimly lit lamps along the ceiling. This man…he was like Athena. "You're a Cognitive," I finally told him.

He paused at the term, turning to face me. His eyes narrowed with a sudden interest. "How do you know what a Cognitive is, Mr.….?"

"Hughes," I said. "And I know because I've met one before. No wonder you know so much about Earth tech. What are you doing in a place like this? Were you in charge of this place before everything went to hell?"

"You must excuse my ignorance, Mr. Hughes," said Janus. "Could you please enlighten me as to which Cognitive it was that you met?"

Shit, I thought, immediately realizing my mistake. I'd almost said too much. The less these people knew about Athena and *Titan,* the better. I still didn't know if I could trust them, Cognitive or not. "I can't remember her name, but it doesn't matter. The real question is why you're here and who the hell these people are."

"Let us reconvene in the outer hall, please," said Karin.

"Yes, I agree," said Janus. "It would not do the children well to overhear such matters. Come, Mr. Hughes, and I shall attempt to fill in the gaps as best I can."

I nodded. "I guess that'll have to do."

"So what's the story?" I asked the second we were out in the hall.

Janus smiled at the question. "I have to say, Captain, I appreciate how inquisitive you are."

"Information keeps you alive," I said, thinking about the animals I had seen in the caves. "You know what it was that turned this place upside down, then tell me."

"Very well," said the Cognitive, turning to the nearby door. He approached it, glancing back at me. "Inside, please."

I watched him walk straight through the metal and into

the adjacent room. "Does he always show off like that?" I asked, looking at Karin.

Abby, Karin, and I followed Janus into the room, closing the door behind us. I instantly recognized the design of this place, it was so similar to the rooms on *Titan*. The walls were made of the same metallic tiles, which suggested they could be used to show off images and video. At the center, there was a table, although it wasn't quite as pristine as the one we used back on the ship. Instead, there were chipped and cracked corners, and several of the seats had been replaced or removed. "Sit, please," said Janus once we were all inside.

We all sat across from him, each of us beside the other, facing the wall, which flickered to life for a brief moment before going black.

I was about to say something, when I realized this wasn't an accident or a glitch. The image zoomed out, showing stars in the distance, surrounded by darkness. It was the same trick Athena had pulled when she turned the walls into screens, only these were cracked and old, no doubt worn from years of exposure to the elements.

"Do you know the story of Earth?" asked Janus after a moment.

"The Transients left," I said, getting straight to where I thought this lecture was about to go. "The rest stayed behind."

"Ah, so you're aware of that much," said Janus. "Good. It saves me some time." He flicked his wrist and the display changed, showing a planet. Despite never having visited Earth, I recognized it when I saw it, probably from all those pictures Freddie had shown me.

"Most of the Eternals population remained on Earth, while the Transients departed for their own sections of the galaxy," explained Janus. "Not long after the colony ships left, the leadership agreed to begin their own colonization efforts. This was done in order to secure our borders, due to the recent dispute between the two sides."

"I thought all that was taken care of," I said, remembering how the Transients, my ancestors, had left Earth in order to start their lives over. They'd only wanted the chance to work and survive.

"It was," said Janus, nodding. "However, Transient individuals are short-lived, existing for only a century or less. The Eternals knew how later generations might forget the peace their forefathers had fought so hard to achieve, which meant precautions would have to be made to ensure the Earth's security. The Eternals predicted a reverse exodus in the distant future. They believed the Transients would return to claim the planet for themselves, believing it to be their birthright. Because of this, checkpoints and monitoring stations were built all throughout Eternal space, as well as research outposts and colonies. Over the course of five centuries, the Earth's territory was solidified and strengthened, ensuring its survival."

"Is that what this place is?" I asked. "An Eternal outpost?"

"Something like that," said Janus. "It was created to be a mining colony, but a space station was eventually built to safeguard it and a warning beacon placed. I believe that is the signal you detected when you entered the system."

"There was no space station when we arrived," said Abigail.

"No, not anymore," said Janus. "The station broke orbit after a thousand years, crashing far from here, toward the east."

"Did you send anyone to check it out?" I asked.

"No, I'm afraid our ships were far too gone by that point. The…creatures…saw to that."

"Creatures," I said, looking back at Karin. "He's talking about the thing that almost killed us in the caves, right? What did you call them again?"

"Boneclaws," she answered.

Janus sighed, despite a lack of lungs. "A simple name for a complicated problem."

I almost didn't ask, but there was something about the way he said it. "What do you mean by *complicated*?"

"Surely you don't think those beasts have always been here?" he asked.

"Haven't they?" asked Abigail. "Where else could they come from? Did they migrate here?"

Janus flicked his wrist, changing the screen behind him once again, this time to a video inside a facility. It was new and pristine, with people working in the halls. "The original colonists had multiple main projects. Three, to be specific, and each one designated to a separate facility. One involved the development of fusion cores, a small, but exceptionally efficient fuel source. You may have overheard me lecturing my students on them a short while ago."

"Fusion cores?" I asked. "Are those different from Tritium cores?"

He nodded. "Fusion cores are more portable, typically used in handheld devices, such as Lucia's staff weapon, whereas a Tritium core contains enough energy to power an entire facility, such as this one."

"This place has a Tritium core?" I asked.

"Indeed, although it has degraded over time. We've been actively looking for a viable replacement for years."

This gave me pause. If these people had a Tritium core, what other secrets were they keeping?

"As for Fusion cores, they are much more common. But I digress. The other projects were vastly different in scope, decidedly focused more on genetic engineering."

Abigail sat up at the last term. "Genetic engineering?"

"One of the facilities was charged with creating a new type of fauna, specifically designed to clean polluted air. Earth had experienced its share of environmental problems, due to multiple factors, including the conflict between the Transients and the Eternals, but also the development of early Tritium cores," explained Janus.

"Sounds rough," I said. "What's your point?"

He smiled. "Patience, Captain. I'm nearly there,"

assured the Cognitive. "Now, are you familiar with where the Eternals came from?"

I nodded. "I've heard the story. They made themselves immortal." I looked at Karin's white hair. "And they don't get sick."

"Correct," said Janus. "All very true. What you may not know, however, is what came after."

"After?" asked Abby.

"The Eternals had already taken a radical leap forward in human evolution, given their enhanced physiology. They couldn't age or die, aside from any unforeseen accidents, of course. But nothing is perfect. Even the Eternals had their flaws and limitations."

"Here we go," I muttered.

"Indeed," said Janus. "Roughly a century after the Transients departed Earth, the Eternals began to look more closely at their own genetic code. They noticed a sort of degradation taking place. People were not healing as rapidly, and some of the older generation were beginning to show signs of aging for the first time."

"So they really weren't immortal," said Abigail.

"You can imagine the fear," continued Janus. "Panic set in among the leadership as they fought to find a solution. For the first time in centuries, the possibility of a natural death had become real. They couldn't stand by and do nothing, not when they had the full force of the government's science division at their disposal."

"Are you saying that's what the third facility was built for?" asked Abigail. "To find a solution to this?"

He nodded. "Quite so, Ms. Pryar. As you might imagine, the project was a top priority. The public couldn't know about the situation without having a solution in place, so the government moved its research off-world to a separate facility." He paused. "This one, to be exact."

"As in, the one we're inside now?" asked Abigail.

"Correct," said Janus. "Now you might be wondering what any of this has to do with the current state of our little planet."

"The question crossed my mind while you were rambling, sure," I said.

Janus ignored my remark. "The research that was conducted here was unparalleled. Groundbreaking advancements were being made on a monthly basis, largely due to pressure from Earth's government. They wanted solutions immediately, no matter the cost. It was during these experiments that things went horribly wrong." Janus flicked his wrist and the image behind him transitioned to something terrifying—the monster we'd seen in the tunnel. The Boneclaw. "I believe you've had the misfortune of encountering one of these."

I stared at the beast. "Misfortune would be an understatement. They weren't exactly friendly."

"No, they certainly aren't," he said. "Nor are they native to this planet."

"Karin mentioned something about that," Abby said.

"Those scientists made them, didn't they?" I asked, staring straight at the Cognitive. "That's where all of this is going, isn't it?"

Janus frowned, giving me a slow nod. "*We* made them, Captain. I was the Cognitive of this facility. I was given the responsibility to assist the original inhabitants in their research." He turned to look at the monster on the screen, it's snarling face and dead eyes staring off into nothing. "But I failed. In our rush to solve the problem of genetic decay, mistakes were made. Lives were lost. All because we couldn't see the path ahead of us and where it might lead. We used Eternal DNA, experimented with it, hoping to slow the clock."

"What are you saying?" asked Abigail. "That those *things* are——"

"Human," finished Janus, finally saying what I had already suspected. "What you are seeing is the Eternal gene in its purest form. This is where the path to perdition leads, my friends. It is the face of humanity's hubris."

8

AFTER OUR MEETING WITH JANUS, I wanted to get back in touch with the *Star*. It had been four hours since I'd checked in with Siggy. Way too long, I wagered, and I was sure Freddie was going crazy with worry.

"A turn-key," I said, looking at Janus. "You know, an ancient communicator from Earth. You've gotta have a few of those lying around."

"Ah, yes," he said. "If you'll recall, our communications network is down and we are unable to contact anyone outside of this facility."

"You never thought to repair it?" I asked.

"On the contrary, we have made many attempts. The problem is our Tritium core. After two thousand years, it has been nearly depleted, allowing for only minor usage across the facility," explained Janus.

"I take it you don't have a backup," I said.

"Well, the cores are quite rare. There were only three on this planet at the time of the collapse. One for each facility. One went offline many centuries ago, while ours is slowly degrading."

"What about the third?" I asked.

"I'm afraid no one has been able to locate it yet," he explained. "We have someone in the field presently, but I have little hope of a discovery."

I couldn't believe it. There had been three Tritium cores on this world at one time. Three. The effort I'd gone through to procure a single one had been overwhelming. If there was still a core on this planet, even a partial one, the Union would do anything to get their hands on it. All the more reason to cut that signal.

"You'll need to return to the surface in order to establish a connection with your ship, but that shouldn't be a problem," said Janus.

"It took us hours to get here, though," I said.

Karin was standing nearby, talking to Abigail and answering her questions when she perked up at my statement. "We have other ways of moving around," she interjected.

I turned to her. "Oh? You've got a faster way to get us back?"

"Of course. You don't actually think we use those tunnels regularly, do you?" she asked with a light chuckle. "You saw how dangerous they are."

"Why was your mother down there, then?" asked Abigail.

"She was scavenging. Mother hates sitting around. She prefers to stay busy. She says it keeps her active."

"Keeps her active?" I repeated. "I didn't know fighting flesh-eating monsters was the same thing as knitting."

Karin laughed. "I'll be sure to tell her that."

Janus flicked his wrist, changing the screen to show the layout of what I assumed must be the facility in its entirety. A red light blinked on the screen, inside a tiny room. "This is our current location," he said before I could ask. "You'll want to leave and head in this direction."

A line left the dot and went through a series of passages, all the way outside the compound. "I'll be taking you there myself," said Karin.

"Why?" I asked. "It doesn't seem that far."

"We'll have to pass through a tunnel," she explained, walking to the screen and pointing to a gap in the passageways. "Here. I don't expect any danger, but you never know."

"Is this the safest path?" asked Abigail.

"It's the best we have," said Janus. "There used to be multiple tunnels that the Boneclaws avoided, but over the last decade, they've grown more curious. I believe their primary food source has migrated."

"None of that matters," I said, hurrying on with it. "Let's focus on getting us back to my ship."

"Of course," said Janus.

"Please meet me in the hall when you're ready," said Karin. She opened the door. "I need to gather some fighters."

"Could I come with you?" asked Abigail. "I'd like to meet a few more people before we go."

The two women shut the door, leaving me alone with the Cognitive. It only took him a moment to break the silence. "Captain, I have one request, before you leave," he said.

"Of course you do," I muttered. "What is it?"

"You're the first visitors to this planet in nearly two millennia. Why is that?" he asked.

"Why?" I repeated. "I guess it's because you're in the middle of nowhere. There's no direct slip tunnel. The only reason we found you is because we randomly dropped out of one."

"Direct tunnel?" he asked. "I'm not sure I understand."

I leaned against the table and let out a short sigh. "Old Earth ships were able to create tunnels to travel through the galaxy. You probably know about that, since you were around back then, but what you might not know is that the technology to do it was lost. When the early colony ships left Earth, they created a network of slip tunnels, which we've been using ever since. The reason no one has found this planet is because there were no tunnels connecting you to us. That's how I understand it anyway."

"Interesting," said the Cognitive. "You mentioned you fell out of one, is that right? That it broke?"

78

"Someone attacked us and sent a bomb inside the tunnel, breaking it ahead of us," I said.

"Ah," he said, nodding. "I understand. But this means our system is connected to the rest of the galaxy once again, doesn't it? Your people and mine."

"How's that?" I asked.

"The tunnel you fell out of. It's open now, and more could come here if they followed." He flicked his wrist, changing the screen to show the planet we were on, covered in white from pole-to-pole. "What enemies do you have, Captain? Should we be concerned?"

I paused, not knowing what to tell him. Of course he should have been concerned. The Union and Sarkonians were deadly. They'd kill or capture everyone here, take all their technology, and strip the place to the ground, all for better weapons and a chance at building their supposed super soldiers. "Yes," I finally admitted. "I guess you should."

"In that case, Captain Hughes," said Janus. "I believe we should discuss what to do next. Don't you agree?"

"First things first," I said. "I need to shut down that signal."

"Are you referring to the warning message?" he asked.

"The one that brought me here in the first place?" I asked. "Yeah, that's the one."

"I understand. You're worried others might detect it and follow."

I nodded. "That message mentioned Earth. It was the

only reason I came here. If we don't shut it down soon, the Union might find you, and you really don't want that."

"Why, exactly? What makes them different from you?"

"Your people are different from the rest of the galaxy," I explained. "They're unique."

"In what way?" he asked.

"Karin and the others are Eternal," I said. "Isn't that right? White skin, blue eyes, fast healing, perfect genes. I'm not a geneticist, but that's how I understand it."

"You know your history, Captain," said the Cognitive.

"Maybe," I said.

He smiled. "I'm afraid my people are not what you might imagine. They no longer retain the perfect DNA of their ancestors. Quite the opposite, in fact. They live an average lifespan of 150 years. Their healing rate is slightly above average, compared to Transient individuals. They hold little in common with Eternals. Perhaps they fall some-where in the middle."

I paused. "But they're all albino."

"The appearance remains, while the rest has faded over time," he explained. "Lucia is the oldest at 162, but I don't expect her to last more than a few more decades."

I scoffed. "That's still pretty damn good."

"What is the average lifespan of your people, Captain?"

"A century if we're lucky," I said. "130 years, if you've got the money for the replacement parts and gene therapy."

"Pity," he said, shaking his head. "I expected by now

that even Transients had figured out a way to extend their lives beyond 150 years."

"Give it time. The second the Union finds this place, they'll stick each of these people in a lab and dissect them, one pound of flesh at a time."

"Well, then," said Janus. "Let's try to avoid that outcome. Shall we?"

THE HALL WAS damp and cold, much like the rest of this horrible place. I couldn't imagine living here for even a day, let alone a lifetime.

Karin and Abigail were ahead of me, walking together, with several others behind us. Men and women, dressed in scraps of metal armor, each with a staff in their hand. What did they think of me? Did I look like strange to them, the same way they did to me? How often did they get to see someone who didn't have pale skin and white hair? I probably looked like a freak.

This must be how Lex feels, I thought. *Or maybe she's still too young to understand.*

Lucia took the rear, following the rest of us with her spear in hand. She had the look of a quiet warrior, something you didn't see much of, except in the back of an empty bar, where a grizzled soldier might sit alone, drinking and trying to forget. An old warrior from a forgotten war.

I guessed Lucia had never been in a war, not in the traditional sense, but she'd probably had her share of killing. I had little doubt there were ghosts living in those eyes.

Karin was the opposite, and it didn't take much to see why. She was young, and while she'd probably fought her share of battles, she wasn't quite as jaded as the old woman. That kind of thing took time. If she stayed on this planet for the rest of her life, she might turn out the same. Pity.

Pity, I thought, repeating the word in my head. *I'm beginning to sound like Freddie. Sentimental bastard must be rubbing off.*

Janus had asked me to help these people, to find a way to get them off this planet, but until he gave me a solution I could work with, there wasn't much I could do. Despite my better judgment, I wanted to help them. I felt a little responsible for what might happen if the Union showed up and wiped them all out, but I couldn't fix everyone's problems. I was only one guy.

Besides, last time I checked, I had my own stuff to deal with. *Titan* was still out there, probably running around looking for us. If they didn't show up soon, I'd need another plan besides just sitting around this godsforsaken place, waiting to die.

"Stay together," said Karin. She looked at Abby then to me. "You'll be safe in the middle."

"Are you anticipating an attack?" asked Abby.

"Always," Karin answered. "It's the only safe way to live down here, especially when you leave the gate."

"Fair enough," I said. "We'll let you take the lead."

The old metal walls faded into stone and ice as we continued along the path. It was the same thing I'd seen when we first left the warehouse on the upper floor, no doubt created by the Boneclaws.

But if they were this capable, I wondered why they hadn't just invaded these people by now. Were they incapable of breaking through certain areas? Was the compound where Karin and her people lived somehow safe from them?

I pushed the questions out of my head and tried to stay focused on the moment. There would be plenty of time for all this later when it wasn't so dangerous to risk getting lost in your thoughts.

Karin raised a fist as we stepped into the stone tunnel. She paused. We all did, each of us watching her and waiting. After a moment, she lowered her hand and continued forward, the rest of us at her back.

We walked for over an hour, slowly and cautiously, and with good reason. The animals could be anywhere at any time, which meant we had to stay on constant guard. I kept hearing sounds, here and there, throughout the caves and tunnels. A sort of clicking sound, faint and faraway, like it could be anything...or nothing. The entire walk to the surface, I heard those lingering clicks and taps. If I had to stay and live in this place forever, surrounded by these distant echoes, I was sure I'd lose my mind and get lost in it.

By the time we reached the surface, all I wanted to do was get out.

9

As soon as we exited the cave, I heard my comm click and a familiar voice spoke into my ear. "Sir, is that you?" asked Sigmond. "I'm detecting your transmitter. Are you receiving me?"

"Siggy!" I snapped, relieved to hear his voice. "Sorry to keep you waiting, pal."

Abigail and Karin both looked at me, probably surprised by my sudden outburst.

"What are you looking at?" I asked them, cocking my brow. "Anyway, Siggy, we're good. Found ourselves a couple of friends, but we're almost back. Tell Freddie to meet me in the cargo bay."

"Excellent, sir. Shall I prepare some coffee for you?" asked the A.I.

"That'll do just fine," I said, imagining the warm aroma, letting my mouth water at the thought.

The *Renegade Star* was exactly where I'd left it, parked in the middle of a white field, snow falling all around it.

The lift door lowered and I hurried my way inside the ship. Freddie was running down the stairs at the same time, while Abigail and I hurried to meet him. I couldn't let Karin or the others stay out in the blizzard, so I invited them inside.

"Welcome back, Captain," said Freddie, relief all over his face.

Dressler was right behind him, standing at the top of the stairs. "Who...Where did you find those people?" she asked, looking across the bay at Karin's people.

The white-haired natives walked beside the shuttle from *Titan* that I'd parked in here after the last battle. It no longer powered on, since we were so far from Athena and her moon, so until *Titan* returned to pick us up, the shuttle was little more than a paperweight.

"I found them in the caves," I said to Dressler as I began to climb the stairs.

She didn't look at me but kept her eyes on the natives. I could tell she was studying them, trying to take in every detail. No doubt, she'd already noticed the obvious: that they looked exactly like Lex and Athena, with white hair, blue eyes, and pale skin. Maybe she'd already picked out the tattoos on them. The woman was more observant than she let on. It was a shame she never became a Renegade.

"See something you like?" I asked her as I approached.

She finally looked at me. "Are these people—"

"Let's save the theories until we're alone, Doc," I whispered, motioning to the door.

She nodded slowly and said nothing else about it. All those years of working in a Union lab and keeping secrets had evidently paid off. Dressler knew how to shut up.

"Stay here," I told the natives once we were in the lounge. "Try not to touch anything."

"This is your ship?" asked Karin, ogling the design. "Strange."

"Better, I think you mean," I said.

"No, that's not it," she said. "It just looks so different from what we have. Like that." She pointed to the nearby coffee maker. "What is it?"

Of all the things she could have told me, her ignorance of coffee crushed my heart the most. *You poor sheltered fool*, I thought, but then said, "I'll show you later."

Abigail leaned against the wall, next to the couch. "I'll stay with them while you debrief with Frederick and Dressler."

"If you want," I said, shrugging.

Karin's soldiers sat on the couch and sofa chairs, looking completely out of place. I could tell they didn't know what to make of any of this, probably because it wasn't a giant ice hole in the ground. I just hoped they didn't get used to it.

Not that I had any finer things to give them, but when

you spent your entire life surviving on scraps, something as simple as a couch probably seemed like a hot commodity.

I nudged Freddie and Dressler into the cockpit, closing the door behind me. I could sense their confusion, especially Freddie, who had that bewildered expression on his face that I had seen all too often.

"Before either of you ask, the answer is yes. I'm totally fine," I said, leaning up against the wall.

"That's not what I was going to ask you," said Dressler.

"Oh," I said, frowning at the doctor. "And here I thought you were concerned about my well-being."

She ignored my sarcasm. "What I want to know is where all these people came from, why they look the way they do, and why you decided to bring them all back to the ship."

"That's a lot to unpack," I said, waving her off.

"How about you start from the beginning," she suggested. "What happened when you went into that cave?"

AFTER EXPLAINING everything I'd seen in the caves to both Dressler and Freddie, they just stared at me. "What is it?" I asked them. "You didn't like my story?"

"Are you telling me that there are blind animals down there capable of burrowing through solid rock?" said Dressler, a look of disbelief on her face. "And that they are somehow genetically altered human beings from experiments that were performed hundreds of years ago?"

"More or less," I said.

"Well, that's just crazy," she said, rolling her eyes.

"You know, you'd think someone who spent their time screwing around in a lab would be a little more open-minded," I said.

"That is precisely why I doubt your story, Captain," said Dressler. "However, I'll humor you on this. If what you're saying is true and these people are telling you the whole truth and not a fabrication, then it changes everything, particularly about those animals."

"How do you mean?" asked Freddie.

"Well, we're talking about genetically engineered humans, correct?" she asked. "That implies they may retain some level of basic intelligence. More importantly, it raises the question of what the Union might do should they come into contact with these creatures."

"Dissect them, I'd imagine," I said.

She nodded. "There's also the matter of there being an entire race of people on this planet who appear to hold a particular set of genes, the likes of which have only ever been seen in the DNA of a small girl." She cleared her throat.

"I'm surprised, Doc," I said, examining her. "You finally letting go of all that Union brainwashing?"

She scoffed. "I'm not brainwashed, Captain. I'm simply aware enough to know how zealous the military is. They want better soldiers, more data, and bigger guns. They'll do whatever it takes to make that happen, even if it means killing all of these people."

I had to admit, Dressler's sentiment caught me off guard. She seemed the cold, scientific type. Someone who wouldn't have a problem experimenting on a living person if it meant more knowledge along the way.

"I know how desperate the government is to acquire additional resources. The Union is, like any other large government body, intent on securing its borders and protecting its citizens. Doing so requires them to seek out and acquire whatever tools they can." She sighed. "I'm not *particularly* fond of the war machine, despite my role in it. Violence might be necessary sometimes, but if I can avoid it, then I'm happy to do so."

I leaned back, crossing my arms. "What are you trying to say?"

"That sometimes soldiers get carried away," she finally said. "They stop thinking about long-term consequences and focus on the present. But I'm in the business of objectivity, and right now, I see a group of people who don't deserve to have their bodies ripped apart and studied in a lab."

I stared at her for a moment. Dressler wasn't a fool, it seemed. Sure, she still couldn't shake her union loyalties, but at least she had the intelligence to see the dangers here. She knew what powerful men would do with powerful things, and it scared the hell out of her.

"Are you saying you'll help me?" I asked.

"If it means saving all of these people, then I'll do my duty," she answered. "Not for you, and not for the Union, but for *them*."

"That's good enough for me."

I DECIDED it would be a good idea for us to get Siggy patched into the network and download all the information we could find in the facility.

"That should not be a problem, sir," said Sigmond. "I only require a series of repeater stations between the *Renegade Star* and the network interface."

"How many do we have?" I asked.

"Approximately eight devices," informed Sigmond.

I clasped my hands together. "I guess that'll have to do."

Freddie was standing right next to me, listening to the entire conversation and waiting for orders. "I'm surprised you have something like that on the ship," he said, after a moment.

"You'd be surprised how many times I have to do this kind of thing in my line of work," I explained. "Just five months ago, I stole some data from an arms dealer. It was a bit like this, with me running underground, carrying network repeaters and dropping them as I went. Of course,

I didn't have to deal with any messed-up animals or a bunch of albinos, but whatever. Close enough."

"I'm just glad you know what you're doing, Captain," said Freddie.

"*Me?*" I balked, opening the locker and removing several of the repeaters. "*You're* coming with me. Or did you really think you were going to get to sit all of this out?"

He looked startled. "I, uh, I guess I thought you didn't want me getting in the way."

"In the way?" I asked, stuffing the repeaters in a small bag and handing them to Freddie.

He took them, wrapping the bag around his belt.

"Someone has to carry all this shit. I wasn't kidding with you about those Boneclaws, Fred. I need to keep my gun out."

He swallowed. "O-okay, then."

I opened another locker and retrieved a rifle, handing it to him. "Just in case," I told him.

"Right," he said, strapping it to his back. "I'll do my best."

10

I HAD Abby and Karin gather everyone together on the upper level of the cargo bay after Freddie and I were done.

Naturally, I restocked my ammunition, since I used most of it in the last run. Once Abby showed up, she did the same, exchanging her magazines and even replacing her pistol with a rifle. We'd need all the firepower we could get if we ended up running into another Boneclaw.

"Are you certain you want to go down there again?" asked Karin. "My men might not be able to protect all of you." She glanced at Freddie.

"We'll be fine," I told her. "Besides, Janus promised you'd look after my crew, so you'd best not screw it up."

"He mentioned saying that," she said. "Along with the reason you need to go there."

"Then you know what's at stake," I said.

She nodded. "The safety of my people, which you've endangered by being here."

"I can leave right now if you want. We'll see who else shows up. Maybe they'll be nice. Who knows?"

"Easy, Jace," said Abigail, walking up beside me. "Just do the job and try not to be such an ass about it."

"Mind who you're calling an ass, lady," I scoffed.

Dressler, Freddie, Abigail, and I joined the natives in the open field after a few moments. We were all geared and ready, each of us armed, with the exception of Dressler, who I still didn't completely trust. I was pretty sure she understood. After all, she still didn't trust me either.

I ordered Siggy to close the gate and seal the ship behind us. If anything went wrong and we didn't show back up in the next 24-hour period, Siggy had my permission to take off into space and wait for Athena to show up with *Titan*.

I hated making contingency plans. It always meant I had to think about the possibility that I might not come back. That thought was horrifying.

We stomped our way through the snow, one step at a time. The cold wind nipped at my cheeks, stinging harder than I liked.

Shortly after re-entering the cave, using the same entrance Abigail and I had first come through, I looked at Karin and asked, "How often do you people come here?"

"There's not much reason to anymore," she explained. "All the good resources have been taken out by now. We've had to expand our scavenging efforts to the outer compartments, although even those have yielded fewer results in recent years."

"I guess that's bound to happen after you spend hundreds of years trying to live on scraps," I said.

"Believe it or not, there was a time that this facility was filled with highly advanced technology. Janus has shown me images and recordings that make it look unbelievable," she said, her eyes drifting.

"Yeah, well, it's all gone now," I said right as we entered the first warehouse.

Abigail climbed down the ladder, followed by Freddie and Dressler, and then me. Dressler seemed to want to explore, but I'd already been there and done that. "There's nothing to see here," I told her. "The good stuff is down that way." I pointed to the gaping hole in the wall.

She stopped, her eyes widening at the destroyed brick and metal. "Did one of those *creatures* do that?"

"What do you think?" I asked, walking past her and into the tunnel.

I could almost feel the fear in the air, mostly from Freddie and Dressler. They had to be concerned about what we might find, but with so many soldiers at our side, I was pretty sure there was nothing to worry about.

After a while, Karin informed me that we were drawing

close to the nesting grounds of the Boneclaws. I noted that we were also near the weird little piles of bones that Abby and I had found. "Stay on alert," she said, looking at her team. "Keep your ears and eyes open."

We passed through the bones soon enough, but this time, they were different. This time, several had been scattered, no longer neatly stacked.

I could see by Karin's expression that this was unusual, possibly even bad. She didn't say anything, so I left it alone, but I wasn't an idiot. I knew this wasn't normal.

Karin tightened her grip on the staff. We moved swiftly, passing into the section with the lit-up consoles.

Freddie and I had placed five of the seven repeaters by this point, each one nestled between rocks or against the wall. I hoped that doing so would keep them hidden away from any of the animals that might pass through.

"Sending verification signal, sir," said Sigmond. He'd been doing this regularly, every few minutes.

I said nothing but felt relief to know the line was still working. Only a little further and we'd have this whole mess sorted out once and for all.

It was about this time that I felt a hand grab my shoulder. I turned to see Dressler staring up at me, a wide-eyed expression on her face. She had her mouth open, like she was about to say something, sweat dripping from her forehead, despite the cold. She raised a finger to touch her lips, then to her ear.

I tried to listen but couldn't hear anything. Neither

could anyone else. Not yet anyway. I was about to ask her what her problem was, when suddenly, I heard a *clank* from somewhere down the tunnel.

Everyone stiffened but immediately raised their weapons, pointing in the direction of the sound.

We each sat there, hardly breathing.

Another sound, similar to the first, echoed through the darkness.

That was when I felt the ground tremble, the way it did the last time I saw a Boneclaw. *This is it*, I thought, clutching my rifle.

I stared down the barrel, aiming at the edge of the wall, near the tunnel. A shadow appeared, moving gently against the farthest wall as the animal rounded the corner. I saw white fur and a black nose. It was a *tiny* animal with long ears and whiskers. It bounced from its hind legs, hopping forward before stopping to look at us.

I felt the tension in the air dissipate, and each of us breathed sighs of relief.

One of the soldiers let out a nervous laugh. "Only a synx," he said.

The little creature hopped again, twitching its nose and whiskers.

I started to ask what a *synx* was, when I felt another tremor beneath my feet.

Ahead of us, I heard something grunt, there in the next room.

I turned, slowly, hoping I was wrong.

The dead eyes, or lack thereof, of another Boneclaw stared back at me. It was hunched over and standing in the doorway.

Staring at the monster, I reached over and touched Abigail's shoulder. She turned, looking terrified. Everyone raised their weapons.

Karin held a fist up, and everyone waited.

The monster paused, twitching its ears.

Karin lowered her hand and the other soldiers fired, hitting the animal across its body.

The Boneclaw let loose another cry and came charging, sweeping its long claws against the metal floor.

The room filled with a loud grind, the noise piercing my ears and making me cringe.

I aimed my rifle and fired a spray of bullets. They hit the animal's rough hide, but only a few shots pierced its skin.

The Boneclaw kept coming, despite all our firepower, snarling and spitting.

A sudden blast of blue energy split the animal's side, spilling guts and blood onto the cold floor.

Drops of it hit me in the face, but I ignored it and focused instead on reloading. The animal wailed loudly, filling the entire facility with noise. Between that and the gunfire, I could only imagine how many of these things had heard the commotion.

The animal collapsed, holding itself up with one arm,

digging its claws into the floor before swiping blindly to the side, no doubt in frustration. Its arm slammed into one of the consoles, ripping and tossing it several meters behind.

Lucia took a step forward, towards the beast, and fired her staff a final time. The blast struck the animal directly in the stomach, finally killing it.

The victory was short-lived. Several more screams echoed through the compound, coming from all directions.

"We need to move!" I snapped, knowing what was about to happen if we stayed here.

"Where?!" asked Freddie.

Karin pointed in the direction the animal had come. "Inside! Hurry!"

No one argued, and we all ran together into the next corridor. I heard stomping coming from behind us, and tremors ran through the floor like a stampede. I let the others go first and held the rear. As Lucia and Freddie passed me, I turned back to see several shadows appear in the same place the tiny animal had been. A second later, the first of them rounded the corner—another Boneclaw, followed by two others.

It clutched the bouncing creature in its jaw, biting down on it with a loud snap. Blood ran from its mouth and neck as it stood there, head tilting, a blank stare in its dead eyes.

I turned and ran further into the dark, away from the nightmare behind me.

They wailed, echoing cries filling the tunnels. The

ground trembled as the creatures followed. It felt like the building might collapse in on itself, but I didn't look back.

One of the soldiers tumbled forward, falling on the floor in his hurry to escape. I nearly ran right over him, but at the last second managed to leap out of the way. He struggled to get back up, so I grabbed him by the arm and pulled. "Get up! Get up!" I shouted. "Move!"

He scrambled onto his feet, joining the rest of our team as we piled into the next room. Karin already had her hands on the door, ready to close it the second we were inside.

She started to push, even before I was through. I turned around and grabbed the edge of the door, then pushed. On the other side, the animals were running our way, screaming their ear-splitting cries. Right before we shut it, I caught a glimpse of the Boneclaw's face, close enough I could have reached out and touched him.

The door locked in place with a loud snap, and the light turned red. The animals slammed into it, pounding against the metal with their heavy fists.

"That isn't going to hold!" shouted Lucia.

"What are you talking about?" asked Dressler. "Did you see how thick that door is?"

"Not thick enough!" snapped Abigail, who had already seen what these animals could do.

"Right!" said Karin. "Keep moving, all of you!"

We did as she said and fled further inside, leaving the creatures as far behind as we could. They'd eventually break through, but it would take time. Long enough for us to get to where we had to go, to put space between us.

Karin led us through a winding corridor and around to another large room, this one with dozens of active machines, consoles, and frozen equipment.

It had been a while since I dropped the last repeater, so I set one behind a nearby workstation, out of sight. "Sigmond, are you hearing me?"

"I read you, sir," he answered in a slightly distorted voice.

"That's no good," I muttered, but I knew there was nothing I could do about it. We had gone so far down into this place that even the repeaters couldn't keep the signal strong enough. I had to keep going and hope that the final repeater would be enough, once we reached the goal. "Karin, how much further?"

"Another hall or two," she told me, waving for everyone to keep up.

We started to move, but a sudden pound shook the room, rattling my knees. I stopped, slowly looking back at the locked door.

Another thud, quickly followed by several more, and each was louder than the last, each vibration stronger in my chest.

The door bent with the last hit.

Uh-oh!

The metal ripped from its hinges and fell against the

floor, sending a hard gust of air and deafening noise throughout the room.

On the other side, four Boneclaws stood together, roaring spit and showing their teeth. They were bigger than the doorway, but I knew that wasn't going to stop them.

I took a step back.

The beast snarled, digging claws into the doorway trying to squeeze through. The others screamed, pushing the first one so hard, it began to whine from the pain.

I didn't even bother to fire my weapon but bolted in the opposite direction instead. I was a man possessed.

I entered the nearest hall, hearing metal straining behind me as the animals broke through the door. Several yelps came, followed by stomping feet.

"Move your asses!" I yelled as I ran, spotting the rest of the team ahead of me. They seemed to be struggling with another door, trying to swipe the access pad without success.

"It won't let us in!" said Freddie.

"Blast the damn thing open if you have to!" I shouted, still a few meters away.

Another hallway was connected to this one, nearby, branching to the left. "We can take this way," insisted Dressler.

"Wrong way," said one of the soldiers.

Before anyone could argue the point further, the access pad activated. "I have it!" Karin snapped.

The door slid open and the team began to run inside.

Before I could move, Lucia looked at me with horrified eyes. "Get down!" screamed the old woman, lifting her staff to the ceiling.

I didn't have to look behind me to know what she was seeing.

Lucia released a single shot from her staff, just above the Boneclaws.

The rocks came tumbling down, along with metal support beams. Clouds of dust erupted from the blast, blowing towards us and filling my eyes and mouth.

The nearby door slammed itself shut, the access pad switching from green to red, although I lost sight of it in all the commotion. The air was too thick to see much of anything.

Chunks of the ceiling continued to fall around us. I pushed myself back, closer to the wall. When the noise finally subsided, an air of silence fell over the passageway.

"Jace!" Freddie yelled from the other side of the door. "Captain, can you hear me?!"

"I'm here! Stay—" I immediately started coughing from the dust, covering my mouth with my sleeve. It took me a moment to settle down. "Stay back!"

"Mother!" cried Karin. "Mother, are you okay?!"

I leaned forward, trying to find Abby or Lucia. I blindly searched with my hands, touching a large chunk of ceiling.

"...Jace...?" I heard a faint voice say.

"Abby? Keep talking," I told her.

"Where are you? Why can't I see anything?" she asked.

I followed her voice, crawling over rocks and debris before finally touching her arm. She clutched my wrist and slowly sat up. "Are you okay?" I asked immediately.

"I-I think so," she said, but I could hear the uncertainty in her voice. She would need a moment to collect herself.

"Stay still," I said, running my hands down her body, searching for....well, I wasn't sure. Blood, wounds, a piece of metal sticking out of her stomach. Anything that might be a problem. My thoughts raced in a hundred different directions. I felt panic in my chest, a swell of heat in my cheeks.

But there was nothing. No sign of injury that I could find. A sudden wash of relief came over me as I realized she was okay. Thank the gods I didn't believe in.

"Wait here, all right?" I said to her, taking her hands and placing them in her lap. "Don't move."

"Okay," she muttered, still disorientated.

I eased myself off Abby and began moving closer to the larger pile of rocks. "Lucia?" I said, listening for a response. After a brief pause, I continued along the floor.

A muffled yelp came from far away, probably from the other side of this small avalanche. The Boneclaws were likely either dead or injured. I was sure they'd find a way to break through, but not yet. Not with half the tunnel collapsed like this.

"Ugh…" muttered a soft voice from somewhere in the dust cloud, which had already begun to settle.

I followed the sound, edging my way closer. "Lucia?" I asked. "Can you hear me?"

"T-tokalo," she whispered.

I was finally able to see movement through the dust, and I found a hand reaching out of the rubble. It was Lucia, half buried, her staff resting beside her.

I scrambled closer, quickly noticing the smell as I neared. Blood, and it was all over her neck and arm, dripping onto the floor. I tried not to show my concern. "There you are," I said.

She licked her lips, blood pooling out of her mouth. "Takalo bento sin," she said.

"I don't understand," I said, turning to the door behind us. "I found Lucia, but she's speaking in another language!"

There was a long pause. "Karin says the translator is out of range," answered Fred.

"Dolo," muttered Lucia. She reached for her pocket, pulling out a device. It was yet another translator, I realized. Lucia touched the center of it, causing the machine to light up. She brought it towards me. "Here."

"That's better," I said. "You understand what I'm saying now?"

She gave me a slight, shaking nod.

"Good," I told her, placing the device in my pocket. "Try to stay still. We'll get you out of here."

"N-no time," she muttered. "You need to go."

Abby was moving behind us. She was back on her feet again, finally out of whatever shock the explosion had put her in. "Lucia?" she asked, coming up beside me. She started to say something but stopped, probably seeing the state of the old woman.

"We're not leaving," I said.

"The Boneclaws will move the stone. They…they always do," Lucia whispered.

"There's plenty of time before that happens," I said.

She shook her head, but then coughed. Blood sprayed from her lips. "M-my staff," she said, reaching blindly beside her.

I grabbed the weapon and brought it closer to her. "Here," I said.

"Thank you," she whispered.

"Jace, how are we going to get her out of here?" asked Abby. "The door is sealed."

"The other passage," said Lucia. "Go that way."

"What's down there?" I asked.

"The only…" Her voice began to drift. Her eyes closed a little, like she was falling asleep, and she snapped them open again. "The only way out."

"Hey, lady, you gotta stay awake, okay?" I said.

"Karin," she said softly.

"She's in the next room. You'll see her in a few minutes," I said.

I wrapped my hands around a piece of debris, which had fallen on the old woman's belly. I pulled, surprised by the weight, but managed to toss it behind me with a loud thud.

Lucia tensed as I removed several smaller pieces from her legs. "We need to get going," Abigail said, looking up at the wall of rubble between us and the animals.

I could hear the scratching from the other side. The Boneclaws were already moving again. I guessed they hadn't actually started their burrowing yet, but it probably wouldn't be long. Gods knew what they were waiting for, but I didn't want to sit around to find out.

"Karin, Freddie, you hearing me?" I barked. "Any word on getting that door open?"

"We're still working on it," said Dressler. "Karin's codes aren't working, so I'm trying to disengage the lock manually."

"Well?" I asked. "How's that going?"

"Not well," she said flatly. "The system locks down in the event of an emergency. It will take some time to get this open."

More scratches. Stronger and louder than before.

"We don't have time," said Abigail.

"And we're not waiting," I said. I took the old woman's hand. "I hope you're ready to get out of here, lady."

"Where are we going?" asked Abby.

I glanced at the other doorway, the only path left to take. "Karin, where's this other tunnel lead?"

A short pause. "That's where the plants are," Karin answered. "There's a tunnel that can take you out to the surface, but it's not easy to get to…and it's very dangerous."

"We'll have to take our chances. Meet us up top and

bring a stretcher!" I looked down at Lucia. "Time to go, lady."

"D-don't be stupid," she said. "Leave me here and—"

"Shut up," I said, pulling her up and wrapping her arm around my neck. "Ain't none of us dyin' today."

11

ABIGAIL and I carried Lucia as we raced down the darkened corridor, getting as far away from the Boneclaws as possible. Behind us, I could hear rocks and debris tumbling over as the animals dug into the fallen wall. They'd make their way through soon enough and there would be little we could do to slow them.

We rounded a corner and came to a stop when I found another hole in the wall. I assumed that, like the others, this one had also been created by the animals. That meant they could be anywhere in here, not just behind, but all around this area. I cursed under my breath but pressed on anyway, determined to find a way out.

A minute later, we came to a platform in a large warehouse. I shined my light around, discovering quickly that the room opened up into a massive tunnel with two lanes large enough for vehicles to traverse, like an underground highway of sorts. There were no other paths but this one, so we pressed on, heading deeper in.

Lucia wheezed and coughed as we went. I kept looking at her face, only to see blood dripping from her mouth and nose. "We'll set you down in a few," I told her. "Hang in there, all right?"

She answered with another cough, but it was good enough. With her staff strapped to my back, Abigail and I wrapped her arms around our shoulders and carried her between us. The whole process made the journey slower, but I wasn't about to leave her to die of her wounds in a cave or mauled to death by a bunch of bloodthirsty animals. I'd sooner shoot her myself than let that happen.

I noticed the tunnel we were walking through was longer than the others, taking us further away from the previous area. I tapped my ear, trying to open a channel. "Siggy, can you hear me?"

No response. I wasn't even getting a broken voice on the other end. We must have been too far away from the last repeater, and I didn't have any more to place. There was only one left, and Freddie had it.

Not that I minded. He needed it to complete the mission. Siggy would have to hack into the system and shut down the signal. That was more important than anything. If the Union or the Sarkonians came through that slip tunnel and heard that woman speaking, talking about Earth, we'd all be screwed.

I'd have to make do with what I had. No help from anybody. Only me, a nun, and a broken old woman.

Whatever. I'd done more with less before.

"How far does this tunnel go?" Abigail asked after only a few minutes.

"Looks like a while," I said. "Karin mentioned that this direction would take us to another compound. Probably one of the other facilities Janus mentioned."

"Other facilities?" Abigail asked.

"He said there were three of them," I explained. "One for each of the major research projects they were working on before this whole place collapsed and went apocalyptic."

"I remember," Abby said. "One for fusion cores, one for fauna, and one—"

"For Boneclaws," I finished. "At least, that's what they ended up with."

We continued through the giant tunnel, carrying the old woman between us. We kept passing openings in the wall where the animals had broken through from adjacent passages. I kept thinking that we were going to get ambushed at any moment, but it never happened, and the Boneclaws from before didn't seem to be following. Maybe they had a harder time breaking through the rubble than I thought or maybe they'd focused their attention on getting through the door to Freddie and the others.

For now, all I could do was keep going. I'd just have to hope that the others had found their own way out.

THE TUNNEL LED into another warehouse, similar in design to the first. There were pallets and broken equipment scattered all throughout the area, but I could already see the door on the other side, and it was closed. Locked too, by the look of the nearby screen.

I touched my hand to the wall, once we had reached it, and the device activated. My tattoos glowed with a soft blue in response, and I entered the same code I had seen Lucia use.

2-0-1-1-9

The door cracked open, and the warm air beyond struck me. It smelled…strange, like the ground after a long storm.

I ignored it. "Inside, come on," I ordered.

Abigail and I shuffled into the next room and closed the door behind us, locking it.

My pad illuminated the space before us. It was another connecting corridor, but very different from the others. The walls were covered in…vines?

Abigail eased the old woman to the floor. "Hold on a second," she said, going to look at the vines. "What is this about?"

"They look like plants," I said.

"Obviously," she said, not hiding her tone. "What do you think caused this to happen?"

"Is that a serious question?" I asked.

"Why wouldn't it be?" she asked.

"The last area had literal monsters in it, all because a bunch of idiot scientists got cocky," I told her. "I'd bet a thousand creds that's exactly what happened here too."

"The chances of both experiments getting out of hand seems unlikely," she said.

I shrugged. "Maybe when the Boneclaws broke out, this place went to hell too. Without anyone to manage the plants, they probably just got out of hand."

Abigail stared at me. "I guess that would make sense."

I fanned my hand at her. "Anyway, since this door's still standing, I'm betting those animals haven't bothered with this place yet. We're probably safe."

"Unless they're using more of their own tunnels."

"We'll keep an eye out," I said, then nodded to Lucia. "Hey, lady, you doing all right?"

"Worry about yourself," said Lucia before letting out a rough cough. "I'm fine."

"Sure you are," I muttered, picking her legs back up.

Abigail took her by the arms and we lifted her and kept going.

The vines on the wall grew thicker and more dense as we walked deeper into the facility. I spotted a small patch of roots cracking through the floor in the corner. The plants must have been inside the walls and floors, all throughout this compound.

I wondered how deep and expansive these plants were. Had they completely surrounded this facility? It seemed that way. The only question I had was how they'd grown so much without any sunlight to draw from.

I was no scientist. I didn't have the experience or the knowledge to understand what any of this meant or how this had happened. My best guess was that a scientist developed something that could survive in the dark. Hell, maybe these things adapted on their own, since it had been a few thousand years.

But at the end of the day, none of it mattered. Right now, I had to focus on getting out of this place and back to the surface. My questions would have to wait.

We managed to get through two rooms before we finally found a barrier. The door to the next area had been overrun with vines, thick as the wall itself. I didn't have a machete on me, and I didn't expect my gun would do the job either.

I tried to pull the plants apart, but they wouldn't budge. They were stiff and tightly bound. "Damn," I said, not knowing what to do.

"Don't you have a knife?" asked Abigail.

"Sure," I said, pulling out a small ten-centimeter blade. "But I don't think this will be enough. We'll be here for hours, cutting our way through."

"It's better than doing nothing," she answered.

Lucia looked up with her tired eyes. "Use the staff."

I glanced down at the old woman as she lay there, cradled between us. "The staff?" I asked. "I don't know how to use that thing."

"You have the marks," she explained. "Point and fire."

Abigail twisted her lips. "Is that a good idea? The last time that weapon was used, it brought down the ceiling."

"The boy can handle it," said Lucia.

I motioned with my chin to the back corner of the room, telling Abigail to move away from the door. We sat Lucia down, and I took a few steps back, grabbing the staff with both my hands and taking my position in front of the door, halfway across the room.

"Are you sure about this?" asked Abigail.

My tattoos glowed as soon as I wrapped my fingers around the weapon. Instantly, a small light near the trigger illuminated and dimmed. I took aim, already prepared for the knockback, and squeezed the trigger. A blast of energy exploded from the staff, hitting the door dead-center with a thunderous noise so loud, I thought for sure the room would come down on us.

But when the dust settled a moment later, all of us were fine and the path was clear.

I looked at Abigail. "Does that answer your question?" I asked, placing the staff on my back and walking over to Lucia. I looked down at her. "And don't call me 'boy' again, Grandma, unless you want me to leave you here."

She smiled at me. "I like the attitude," she said, then looked at Abigail. "Lucky for you, he's too young for me."

Abby blinked. "W-what does that mean?"

WE HAD to stop after a while. The old woman had started bleeding again and that required some attention.

Abigail handled it. She had enough experience with bandages to temporarily relieve the problem, but it wouldn't be enough for the long-term.

"I just need to rest," Lucia told us. "Please stop and let me sleep."

We'd made it to an area with hardly any plants. It seemed like a decent place to stop, at least for a few hours. We could give the old woman time to rest while the two of us figured out what to do.

I checked the doors, securing each of them in case any Boneclaws decided to drop in. The locks still worked, thankfully, and since none of us planned on making a lot of noise, I didn't expect any visitors to come this way.

For now, we seemed to be safe, although I certainly wasn't about to let my guard down.

"I'm cold," said Lucia once she was lying down.

I removed my coat and placed it across her chest. "That'll do you fine," I said.

She nodded, closing her eyes.

I sat against the wall, near one of the doors. Lucia was

on the other side, already fast asleep. She must have been exhausted, despite the sassy attitude. *Tough little lady*, I thought.

Abby came and sat beside me. We had the pad resting a meter away, filling the old room with a dim glow. It allowed me to see her face, soft light reflecting off her cheek.

"Think you'll be able to sleep?" I asked.

"Not yet. I need to wind down first," she answered, looking at the floor in front of her. "Do you think she'll make it?"

"Lucia?" I asked, glancing over at the old woman, who by now was lightly snoring. "Sure. She's a tough one."

"Maybe," she said. "I just don't want her to die because…because of us."

"She'll be fine, Abby," I responded, trying to reassure her, but not quite knowing how.

She leaned against me, placing her head on my shoulder. I jerked at first, surprised, but settled and relaxed after a second. *She's never done that before*, I thought.

I let my eyes fall on her hair. It glistened in the dim glow, still beautiful despite the amount of trouble we'd found ourselves in.

How had I ended up in this place, here with this woman? I'd always been alone, always tired and sick of people. I never wanted a crew or to be involved with someone else's problems.

Yet here I was, sitting in a cave, holding a nun and telling her everything was going to be okay.

Abigail nestled herself in my chest. It felt right, like this horrible place was exactly where I was meant to be.

I stared down at her, and she fidgeted in my arms.

She turned, looking up at me, saying both nothing and everything, all at the same time.

The hell with it.

I kissed her, pressing my lips into hers…and to my surprise, she kissed me back, wrapping her hand around my neck and running her fingers through my hair. All my thoughts and worries drained out of my mind, like nothing else mattered.

Only the moment. Only the girl.

Finally, we embraced one another, losing ourselves in the dark of that ancient, forgotten place.

12

"I'LL NEVER KNOW what's out there if I don't go," I said, standing on a loading dock in my maintenance uniform, one of only three sets of clothes to my name. The other two were in my duffel bag.

Teddy stood in front of me, wearing the exact same uniform, only he had a gold stripe on his collar with a pin to signify his time-in-service. We were still the same rank, because you couldn't get any higher in maintenance than the rank you started with. There was no upward momentum on this station. Not unless the chief died or retired, but good luck waiting around for that to happen. "You sure you wanna do this, Jace?" he asked in his grizzled voice, placing a hand on his hard, fat belly. I'd seen pictures of Ted when he was my age and knew he hadn't always looked this way, but a few decades of drinking a belly full of booze will stack the weight on if you aren't careful. Not that he cared. Teddy was never one for appearances.

"I can't stay here forever," I told him. "No offense."

He chuckled. "None taken, but it's a hard life out there, and we got long-term security here. I'm up for a pension in another ten years. Not bad for an ex-con, ya know?"

Teddy had a point. If I stayed on Talos, the work would be steady and I'd have the routine, which was more than most could say, but fifty years of labor for a crappy pension just didn't seem as appealing to me. Both Teddy and I had come from Epsy. We'd been sent to Talos through the jobs program, each for different reasons. Teddy had stolen some money thirty-eight years ago, spent five years in prison, and couldn't get a job doing anything but cleaning up after other people. He managed to get in with a good company through a family friend, which eventually got him sent up here. That was about the best he could've hoped for. Not too many people were willing to help out an ex-con.

I was a different case. I'd pulled my share of jobs, but that was when I was still a teen. All it did was get me sent to juvie for six years. When I became an adult and they kicked me out, I was offered a series of low-level assignments. Each of them paid about the same, but only one stuck out. Only one took me off-world.

Even if it meant cleaning toilets and fixing pipes, moving to Talos was a step in the right direction.

"You know I can't stick around. I came here for a reason, and now that I've gotten enough money to—"

"Yeah, I know it, kid," said Teddy. "You ain't gotta tell me. Your daddy was the same way."

I nodded but said nothing. Teddy had known my old man, it turned out, and even worked beside him on several occasions. My dad had come to Talos Station the same way I had—on a shuttle with a job waiting for him. The difference was that he didn't keep his priorities in check. He lost sight of the dream…then went and did something stupid.

But that was my old man. Dead from a bar fight, here on this station, gods rest his soul. He never even made it out of the system.

I wasn't going to make that mistake. I'd saved a thousand creds over the last six years—enough for a new life. I might not be a Renegade tomorrow, but with enough money and time, I'd get what I wanted eventually.

All I had to do was work for it.

"Don't get yourself killed or anything," he said, scratching his ear. "And don't be a stranger either! Don't leave me wondering where you went off to, ya hear?"

"I'll call you on the holo tomorrow," I assured him.

He scoffed, fanning both his hands at me. "You just remember what I told you. When you land, use some of those creds to get yourself a pistol. Can't be running around without protection. It's just a shame you can't take one on the ship." He shook his head at the transport.

"I'll get one, first thing, along with some Bordo

noodles," I said, only half-joking. The food on Bordo was supposed to be great, but Teddy and I had always preferred the simple stuff. No fancy exotic crap for us. One night, over some eight-credit steaks, he'd made me promise to eat a simple meal when I got to where I was going. We ended up agreeing on noodles.

"You better!" he exclaimed, chuckling and holding his belly. "Call me and tell me how they are."

We smacked each other on the shoulder, a stupid gesture we'd picked up from our time with the maintenance crew. "Take care of yourself, Teddy," I told him.

He nodded. "You too, kid. Don't go and fuck your life up."

"I'll try," I answered, tossing my duffel over my shoulder and heading up the ramp. He moved to the far side of the bay, near the hall door, safe enough from the loading platform to watch the ship disembark. He was more sentimental than he gave himself credit for.

I went to the passenger section and stowed my bag. I made certain to get a window seat, all so I could see my first slip tunnel. I'd only seen holo vids before now, but I heard there was no substitute for the real thing.

As for the cabin, it was largely empty. Not too many people left Talos this time of year, so the passenger section was mostly empty, with the exception of a handful of people.

I leaned back in my chair, going over what I would do when I reached Bordo, the place where my new job waited.

I'd heard there was opportunity there, but that was about it. I figured it was better than Talos, and the gal-net said it had the best jobs for guys like me—people who just wanted to get paid and didn't care about *how*.

The faster I could get a ship and start freelancing, the better. That was the only way to become a full-fledged Renegade.

For now, I'd have to contend with finally leaving this star system—something I'd worked my ass off for. I felt tingles in my fingers as the station released its clamps and allowed us to detach from the airlock.

The engines came alive, roaring like thunder in the middle of a quiet night, and we began to move. I watched the station grow smaller in the window while the ship pushed toward the entrance to the slip tunnel, which was on the other side of the system.

After several minutes, I saw the tunnel open, letting in another vessel. It closed within seconds once the ship was inside. When we neared, I felt another vibration as the slip engine kicked in, telling me it was nearly time.

The process of traveling through slipspace was something that had always fascinated me. I'd read up on it through the gal-net, so I'd seen videos, but commentators said those were no substitute for the real thing. I believed them. Nothing compared to seeing something with your own two eyes. I always believed that, ever since I was a kid.

That was why I wanted to see it all.

The tunnel opened and we eased our way closer to the

rift. I could already see the flashing green of the inner walls. I leaned closer to the window, unable to blink or look away.

Our ship entered, leaving the system behind in the blackness of space as we were suddenly consumed by the tunnel. We shot forward, the slip tunnel walls sparkling with white lightning. It looked like magic, like the best drug trip imaginable.

I'd never seen anything so beautiful.

"Pretty spectacular, isn't it?" asked a female voice.

I didn't look away from the window. Whoever it was couldn't be speaking to me. I'd come here alone.

"Hey, you in the jumpsuit. Didn't you hear me?" she asked.

I slowly turned toward her. She was sitting across the aisle, dressed in a fine suit, hair draped across her shoulders, a drink in her hand. "Huh?" I asked stupidly.

"You've never seen one of those, have you?" she asked.

I shook my head.

"I remember my first time," she responded, taking a sip of the drink, which I guessed was some kind of martini.

"I didn't know you could have alcohol during take-off," I said.

She smiled. "Tell me, what's with the outfit?"

"It's my uniform," I said. "Well, it used to be. I'm relocating."

"To where? Bordo?" she asked.

I nodded.

"What sort of work are you looking for that you'd pack up and leave your home system?" she asked.

"I used to work on Talos' maintenance team, but that wasn't a good fit," I said.

She smiled then put the glass down on her tray. "What would a good fit be for a man like you?"

"I want to be a Renegade," I said, not ashamed of my ambition. "That means I need money so I can get my own ship."

"Interesting," she said, letting my word settle in the air before she spoke again. "Are you a criminal? Do you have a record?"

"What?" I asked, surprised by the woman's blunt question.

"It's difficult to find a job if you have a record," she explained.

"I did, back when I was a kid, but it's clean now. They wipe it when you turn eighteen."

"You have a clean record, but you want to be a Renegade? Why is that, exactly?" she asked.

"That's my business," I said.

"Fair enough." She scanned me with her eyes, being quiet for a long moment. It didn't feel sexual, although she was certainly beautiful. It was more like I was being judged or assessed. "So a boy your age, leaving your home for the first time, barely a credit to your name, and looking for a job. All so you can become a Renegade."

"I have money," I said.

"No you don't," she answered.

I scoffed. "How would you know?"

She motioned at me. "You're wearing a uniform from a job you already quit. If you had any money, you've done a fine job of hiding it."

She was right. The thousand credits I'd saved had been used mostly to pay for this trip. I had enough money for a few months' rent, but I couldn't survive without a job for long.

When I didn't answer, she continued. "No money, no job, yet you still have the courage to take a transport to another planet, all with the hope of finding an…opportunity. That speaks to a man's character, don't you think?"

I hesitated but finally nodded. "Sure."

"On that matter, since opportunity is what you're after, how about I save you a bit of time." She took a long sip from her drink and set it back down. "I just so happen to be a recruiter for a particular organization in the market for people like yourself."

"What does that mean? People like me?" I asked.

"Young, single, and hungry for money," she said. "I didn't meet my quota on Epsy, truth be told, and you seem like the right type."

"Is this a joke? We just met ninety seconds ago and you're offering me a job?"

"I have a good eye for talent," she said. "Now, are you interested? There'll be no questions asked, of course, and you can't have any moral objections."

"What kind of job is this?" I asked. "What do you mean by 'moral objections'?"

She raised her brow. "I thought you told me you were willing to do anything for a paycheck. Did you misspeak?"

"N-no, I meant what I said. It's just that—"

"I don't make a habit out of this sort of thing," she said, cutting me off. "I just feel like being charitable today, that's all, and you happen to be at the right place at the right time. You can take my offer now and start earning some real money—not those scraps from whatever bottom-feeder job you happen to find on Bordo—or you can turn back toward that window and stare off into the slipstream and forget we ever spoke. What's it going to be?"

I couldn't believe the luck of it. Was this woman actually telling me the truth? I stared at her for a moment, those serious eyes staring right back. She couldn't be more than thirty years old, but there was an experience about her— something I hadn't seen since I was living on the streets on Epsy. I knew that this was real.

"Well?" she asked, breaking the silence.

I cleared my throat, licking my lips. "How much?" I asked.

She smirked. "Enough."

"Enough…" I repeated, chewing on the word. "Anything else I should know?"

"Not until you're signed on," she said. "It'll be dangerous, but all the best things are."

I considered saying no, but only briefly. It sounded

sketchy, and maybe it was, but I didn't leave Talos just to wind up mopping floors in a train station or fixing pipes in a hotel. I left so I could do something else…so I could be *someone* else. If I didn't take this offer right now, there might not be another.

I leaned toward her, between the aisle. "If the money's good, like you say, maybe I'll do it."

"Excellent," said the woman. She reached out to me. "My name is Eliza Jenson."

"Jace Hughes," I said, shaking her hand.

"It's nice to meet you, Mr. Hughes," she said with a beaming smile. "I very much look forward to working with you."

13

ABIGAIL SHIFTED beside me but didn't wake. We'd fallen asleep together, my arms around her, and for a while, I had forgotten where I was.

I moved away from her, reaching for my pad to check the time. The screen indicated that a few hours had passed since we'd stopped. I wondered how long we had to stay in this place before moving on. Was it too dangerous to wake the old woman in her present state?

Holding on to the pad, I got to my feet, trying not to make a sound. I'd let Abby sleep for a while longer while I stretched my legs.

A soft blue light glowed where the old woman was sleeping. "Boy," said Lucia, her voice surprising me. She held the translator device in her hand.

I approached her, sitting beside her to whisper, "Everything's fine. You can go back to sleep."

"Resting is for the old and the dead," she said, giving me a half-smile. "I'm not ready to be either."

I returned the expression. "I can see that."

"Good thing for you. If you let me die, my daughter might take your head." She nodded to Abigail. "Your woman's too."

I paused. "My *what?*"

"Oh, yes," said Lucia, smiling. "You aren't as quiet as you think, boy."

"She's not my woman," I muttered, looking away from her. It was the first time anyone, including myself, had ever referred to Abigail and me in such a way. It took me by surprise.

"You haven't realized it yet, that's all," she said, shaking her head. "You're slow, I can tell, but you'll catch on eventually."

"Shut up, Grandma," I said, standing up. "You're going senile."

She closed her eyes, letting out a quick chuckle. "Kids," she muttered to herself. "Too blind to see the sun."

ABIGAIL WOKE A SHORT TIME LATER. "We need to get going," I said, quickly handing over her outfit. "Are you ready?"

She took the clothes from me and nodded.

I waited for her to get dressed, saying nothing as I watched her slip her clothes on. When she was ready, we went back to the old woman, who was sitting up for the first time. "Is it time to go already?" she asked.

"We figured you might be bored of sitting in the dark," I told her.

She chuckled. "Tired of lying down, perhaps."

Abigail bent beside her. "Do you know how much longer before we're out of this place?"

"We tend to avoid this place. The way out is ahead, but it isn't easy to cross," she explained.

"We'll find a way," said Abigail.

The old woman scoffed. "We'll see what you say when you see it."

We picked up Lucia by the arms and legs and resumed our trek through the corridors, leaving the room behind. On the other side, we found more vegetation. More vines covering the walls, with sprouts poking through cracks in the floor, and blades of yellow and blue plants hanging from the ceiling.

My pad's light seemed to shimmer throughout the hall as it hit the vegetation. I couldn't help but feel like I was walking into the mouth of an animal. It gave me chills.

"Easy," I said, stepping over some of the plants. I didn't want to accidentally get a foot caught and wind up dropping Lucia and breaking her hip.

We carefully walked through the hall and reached the

next set of doors. I had to use a knife to pry the overgrown weeds from the touch screen on the wall, giving me access to the controls. The door itself was mostly clean, with only a handful of weeds hanging from its crevices.

The door slid open and we walked through, letting it close behind us.

I stopped, immediately taken aback by what I saw next.

There was a massive hole in the floor, almost like a crater, buried in the center of the large room. Inside the hole, I could see countless moving plants, each waving together, all of them somehow uniquely shaped. Below them, a soft light, coming from inside one of the pit's walls. On the other side, I spotted a stairwell, leading up. *That must be it,* I thought.

"What is this?" asked Abigail, balking at the sight before us.

"I told you it wouldn't be easy," said the old woman.

On either side of the pit, there was a small space against the wall, enough room to edge our way across. "We can make it if we're slow and careful," I said.

"It's not that easy," said Lucia.

"You don't think we can cross?" I asked.

The old woman motioned for a small stone, sitting nearby. "Hand me that, would you?"

Abigail retrieved the rock and gave it to her. Lucia tossed it in the direction of the pit, letting it stop less than a meter from the edge. "What was that for?" asked Abby.

"Wait," she said simply.

I heard something move but couldn't see anything. "Do you hear that?" I finally asked. It sounded like water pouring through a pipe.

Lucia raised her finger, pointing to where the stone had landed. "Look."

Before I could respond, I saw it. A vine, moving on its own, reaching out of the pit and moving toward the rock. It curved and slithered, almost like a beast, making for the stone. Finally, as it reached the rock, the vine wrapped itself around it, and dragged the object back into the hole, disappearing into the darkness.

I'd seen plants that moved on their own before, but only in holo vids. There were planets with jungles that moved, trees and plants that attacked unsuspecting travelers, should they come too close. They were rare, sure, but not impossible.

"Are you saying if we get too close, that pit will attack us?" I asked.

"It will do more than that," said Lucia.

I reached for another rock, deciding to test the boundary of this creature—or was it creatures? How many different organisms was I looking at right now? Were all these plants interconnected?

I shrugged, tossing the rock two meters from the edge of the hole.

Again, a vine came out from inside the pit and took the stone, pulling it back inside.

That was one hell of a reach. "Shit," I muttered.

"I know," said Lucia.

I found another stone and tossed it, but this time closer than the other two. It landed, rolling half a meter before stopping.

We waited for the vines to emerge, but they never did. Now we were getting somewhere.

I tried again, tossing a fourth rock, letting it fall the same distance from the pit as the last one. It landed, rolled a short way, and stopped. Again, no vines. Good. I liked consistency.

"Now what? How are we supposed to get across?" asked Abigail.

"Usually, we'd avoid this section of the tunnels," explained Lucia.

I shook my head. "Well, that's out of the question. Do you know how to get through this?"

She nodded. "I've only come through here once before, back when I was far younger than either of you two. Several of my friends and I were attempting to cross the pit. Most of us were fast enough to make it, all except for one. A boy named Chalter. The vines grabbed his ankle and pulled him down."

"Chalter died?" asked Abigail.

"He was taken by the pit. I had already crossed, the plants nearly grabbing my feet, but when he tried to follow..." She took a slow breath. "The plants took him. The rest of us could only watch."

I could sense the old woman's pain at the memory. She

didn't want to be here. Hell, this might actually be the first time she'd been back here since the accident. But that was in the past, and we couldn't just turn around.

"Is there another way?" asked Abigail.

"We can travel to the third facility," said Lucia. "There is another road, similar to the first. There are no plants there."

"And how long would that take?" I asked.

"Another day," she answered. "And there are Boneclaws between us. Another nest."

I considered the option. After all, it might have been better to wait and play it safe, maybe scout ahead for the animals. We had weapons too, so we'd stand a decent chance, but it might get messy. The old woman had already come so close to dying in the cave-in.

No, I wasn't going to trade one dangerous situation for another. I had no idea what I'd find in that tunnel. No idea how many Boneclaws had taken up residence there. But I knew this situation. I could see the danger right in front of me.

"We're crossing," I said, no hint of doubt in my voice.

"How?" asked Lucia. "Do you plan on throwing me across the hole?"

I paused, taking the staff from my backside and turning it in my hands. "Think you can handle this again?"

"What do you mean, Jace?" asked Abigail.

The old woman reached out and took the rod. "I know my weapon," she returned.

"That's good," I said. "Because I need both of you to do exactly as I say."

We strapped Lucia to my back, tying her legs around my waist. Once she was secure, I tried walking a few paces to make sure I was flexible enough to move.

The pad was in the middle of the floor, set to maximum brightness. The light was strong enough to reveal most of the room, but only the highest section of the pit. I could see vines and plants shifting and dancing against the walls of the chasm.

"Are you sure about this, Jace?" asked Abigail. I could tell she was more concerned with me and Lucia than herself. After all, the two of us would have to rely on only a single set of feet to carry us across the divide.

"I'll be fine," I said. "Don't worry."

"I'll protect him," said Lucia, winking at her.

I walked to the right side of the pit, standing slightly beside the third rock that I'd tossed, which still hadn't been taken by the vines. "Ready?" I asked, looking at Abigail.

She nodded, waiting for me to give the signal as she stood near the edge of the room. The cliff was right ahead of her. "Ready," she answered.

Lucia held the staff in her hands, using my shoulder to steady her aim.

I pulled out my pistol. Holding a rifle was too difficult

with the old woman on my back and the staff on my shoulder, but managing a smaller gun allowed for more flexibility. In any case, I'd have to make it work.

I bent my head to see Lucia. "That thing better not hit me when you fire." I paused. "Or cause a cave in."

"Not to worry," she assured me. "I've turned it down to only half-capacity."

"Is that enough to do the job?" I asked.

"These aren't Boneclaws. Half the power should be more than enough to handle things," she said.

I nodded. "Okay, Abigail," I said, raising my voice so she could hear me on the other side of the room. "Wait for the first shot and then move."

"Understood," she said.

Lucia squirmed a little on my back, taking aim at the pit. "Ready," she said.

I took a quick breath. "Do it!"

A blast exploded from the end of the staff, sending a blue burst of energy across the pit and hitting the other side. A large cluster of plants fell from the wall, leaving a gap between the rest.

At the same time, Abigail was moving, heading quickly across the thin walkway adjacent to the wall.

The vines and plants moved inside the pit, reacting to the blast, some of them heading to the newly formed gap. As I'd expected, they were drawn to movement, even when it was dangerous. Pure instinct.

"Again," I said to Lucia.

She gripped the staff and fired a second time, striking the plants, consuming them in a bright blue light.

More of the vines began to move, this time to the second location. Half the pit was reacting to the explosions, all to my relief.

I glanced at Abigail to see her near at the end of the pit, slowing down because of the increasingly narrow path. She was only a few steps from the other side.

Suddenly, a vine stretched out from the pit, heading for her foot. She jerked away, quickly avoiding its grasp.

"Move, Abby!" I snapped, raising my pistol and trying to aim.

The vine continued after her, bending and curving its way along the chasm. At one point, it stopped, pulling back, replaced by another, and then another. In seconds, there were several of them, each one coming from a different direction beneath the base of the path.

"Shoot it again!" I told the old woman.

She steadied her aim and fired again, hitting far below the pit, but not too close to Abigail. We didn't want the vibration to offset her balance and accidentally send her falling.

The plants reacted immediately, pulling away from her and back toward the section of the wall where the shot had hit.

Abigail reached the other side and I felt a relief wash over me.

"It's about time," said Lucia. "I can feel your shoulders relaxing. You were worried."

"Shut up," I said, walking over to where Abigail had started from. "Just get ready to use that stick of yours."

"I'm always ready," she said.

I bent my knees, prepared to run across. With a slow and steady breath, I paused and said, "Okay...now!"

Lucia fired over my shoulder and I took off running. The shot struck below the edge of the pit, close to where she'd hit the last few times. Like before, the plants began moving toward the impact point, instinctually reacting to the vibrations.

I made it to the thin walkway, staying steady as I moved along to the other side. I couldn't put my back to the wall because of the old woman, so I had to keep facing forward. The balancing was more difficult than I anticipated.

Taking another step, I could hear the rustling movements of the plants beneath my feet. The pit had come alive with activity, the vines slithering in unison.

The old woman squeezed my shoulder. "Look out!" she snapped. "Your feet!"

A vine had come above the floor, edging closer to my ankle. I jerked away, bringing my pistol around and firing on the plant.

The bullet tore through the yellow vine, splitting it in half. The plant paused, retracting momentarily before continuing on again. Despite the damage, it seemed largely undeterred.

At the same time, two other vines appeared, each one following the first, making their way to me. "Use the staff!" I barked. "Shoot something!"

Lucia twisted around and steadied the rod. I took the opportunity to fire into the nearby plants, jumping out of their grasp. A blast exploded from the old woman's stick, hitting the far side of the pit. This time, however, the plants beneath me didn't react. They just kept coming.

"Shit!" I yelled, unloading my pistol. The magazine was almost empty now. I couldn't keep this up, but I still had a dozen steps to go before I reached the other side.

"Shoot them, Lucia!" called Abigail. "Shoot the walkway!"

A vine came at me, grabbing my ankle. It tugged hard enough to make me stop, then it squeezed. I felt the pressure build to the point where it hurt.

It pulled my foot out from under me, causing me to lose my place. I fell on my knee, the plant still holding my other ankle. "Shoot it!!" I shouted. "Godsdammit!"

Abigail ran closer to the pit, ready with the rifle. Before she could do anything, I slipped further down the wall until most of my body was below the edge.

Lucia swiveled on my back, ready with the staff. "Hold on!" she yelled.

I reached with both my hands and gripped the edge. "Do it!" I told her.

She pulled the trigger and fired. The blast struck the cluster of vines, a meter away from my leg, ripping them apart instantly. The force of the explosion hit us, pushing me against the wall.

I lost my grip and fell, vines all around me, and the glowing light beneath us growing brighter by the second. I reached out and snagged a vine with my hand but couldn't hold it. Instead, I slipped again and fell, hitting the ground and falling forward.

"Jace!" I heard Abigail cry.

"We're okay!" returned Lucia, who had managed to stay on my back through all the chaos.

I groaned, pushing myself up. The light was brighter now, filling the area in front of me. I got to my feet, noticing I was standing on a ledge inside the pit. Ahead of me, there was a tunnel, massive roots along the walls, inter-woven with the dirt. At the end, the source of the light—a machine, still powered on and active, with roots encasing it almost entirely.

I edged forward, away from the ledge. There were no vines in here, and none seemed to follow, once I was a few meters inside.

The light was bright and gentle, coming from the center of the device. As I neared, I noticed a familiar design. This was a Tritium core, having the same architecture as the one I'd stolen from the Union and replaced on *Titan*. "Holy shit," I muttered.

"What is it?" asked Lucia, unable to see.

I turned around, giving her a better look. She stared at it for a few seconds before finally asking, "What is this?"

"A core," I answered, taking a step closer to it. "A really powerful one."

I imagined the possibilities of having another core, especially considering how difficult the last one was to obtain. When *Titan* found us, we might need a backup power source. Considering one had just fallen into my lap, I couldn't simply walk away, even if I was sitting in the belly of a giant man-eating vegetable.

I stepped closer to the device, examining it closely. The roots had somehow burrowed inside the machine, almost surrounding the core. I took the container by its lid and tried to twist, but it was far too snug in between the roots. Using my knife, I began to cut around it, chipping away the plant—enough to wiggle the core out from its holding place.

It budged, finally, and I managed to wedge it free.

The device dimmed as it came out, the glow of the tunnel dimming, nearly completely, as the machine lost most of its power. Only a few lights remained active, shining in the new darkness.

The roots suddenly trembled, shaking the walls around me. "What was that?" I asked, tucking the Tritium core in my bag.

"Nothing good," answered Lucia, readying her rod. "Whatever you did seems to have—"

Before she could finish, the ground shook, nearly knocking me over. The roots moved in place, pulling dirt from the walls. "Time to go!" I said, stepping away from the machine.

Vines were already coming up from around the tunnel opening. I took my knife and swiped at them, splitting the plants as they continued to come at me.

"Turn me around!" ordered Lucia.

I didn't argue, sweeping my feet to give her a better view. She fired the rod, releasing a wide blast that evaporated the vines around the tunnel.

I ran to the ledge, looking down at the pit, which was covered in moving *things*, each one reacting to our movement.

Abigail peered over the edge at us, a horrified look on her face. I motioned at her, waving my knife. "Is there anything up there you can use to help us?" I asked.

"Hold on!" she answered, disappearing from my view.

I could sense Lucia doing something with her staff. "Is everything okay back there?" I asked.

"I'm altering the settings," she answered.

I slit two stems at the base, severing them. "To do what?"

"To cleanse the wall without causing a cave-in," she said right as she finished. I heard the weapon prime itself, cycling power. "Ready. Now aim me so I can clear a section for us to climb!"

"On it!" I said.

I retrieved my rifle and planted my feet, turning to give Lucia the best shot possible, towards Abigail.

She squeezed the trigger and shot a steady line of blue energy at the wall, slowly moving it down from top to bottom. "This is going to take a few moments!" she said, her voice just above the sound of the weapon.

I waited for any vines to attack, but they seemed more concerned with the chaos Lucia's staff was causing. The plants moved closer to the blast zone, consumed by the energy as it laid waste to the wall.

I glanced over my shoulder to see Abigail popping her head out from above the cliff. She waved at me, showing something in her hand. It looked like a piece of cloth or rope, tied together.

As Lucia finished clearing the wall, I signaled to Abby, letting her know to drop the line. As she did, I felt the floor rumble. "What is it now?!" I snapped.

A wailing cry rang through the cave, hitting my ears like a high-pitched screech, making me flinch. "Down there!" yelled Lucia, pointing to the middle of the pit.

I looked and saw the vines dispersing from the center of the base, moving away and revealing a plant of some kind.

"Move, Jace!" yelled Abigail, throwing the rope.

I caught it then leaped across the divide and planted my feet on the newly cleaned wall. "Fire that stick, Lucia! Don't let those things come after us!" I barked.

She did, and I heard several blasts hit the distant walls of the pit. The vines around us moved away, concerned with the other impacts. This was actually going to work.

With all my strength, I pulled forward, climbing with

Lucia on my back. Abigail held the other end, using her own strength to help get us there faster. We moved quickly, one step after the next, nearly there at last.

I gripped the side of the cliff, throwing my elbow over the edge, followed by a leg. Abigail gripped my arm and yanked me up, but not before something took my leg again. Another set of vines.

Each plant slid around me, pulling me back. One on each ankle, another on my thigh.

"Jace!" shouted Abby. She fired her rifle into the vines, barely able to make a difference as more and more arrived.

I felt myself sliding back, unable to move forward. "Lucia!" I yelled. "Use the stick!"

The old woman swiveled the staff around, nearly hitting me in the head, but finally managed to get a single shot off. It struck two of the vines right as several more appeared, along with the section of the ridge we had just climbed up from.

I nearly fell again but caught Abigail's hand instead. The sudden stop caused the staff to fling free of Lucia's grip, tumbling into the pit and into the chasm below. "No!" cried Lucia, reaching out for it but unable to do anything.

Abigail pulled me up, and I scurried forward and away from the edge.

The three of us bolted for the stairs, and I felt a rumbling sound from behind us. The blast had caused the ground to break, and now it was coming down around the pit. I stopped a few steps away from the stairs, looking back to watch the madness.

It continued around the pit, cracking the floor in several directions, sending the vines into a wild frenzy.

"It's going to fall!" yelled Abigail, tugging my sleeve.

I followed Abigail up the stairs, taking two steps at a time, but paused before I was clear.

Below us, the hole had opened up, and I saw in its belly an entire sea of arms—vines moving beneath the pit itself, rocks and metal chunks falling all around them. At their center, I saw a massive thing—the heart of the pit—opening and closing its sides like a mouth.

A hand gripped my chin. "Go, you idiot fool!" screamed Lucia into my ear. She smacked me hard across my cheek. "*Run!*"

I blinked then pushed the image I'd just seen out of my mind. Without another thought, I ran forward, up the stairs and into the darkness. There was a light, far ahead of us— a crack in the veil.

Abigail arrived first and entered the code next to the hatch. It wouldn't open, which meant we'd have to force it.

I grabbed the manual control and pulled, slowly moving the metal handle from right to left. Abigail pressed against the door with her back and hands, gritting her teeth as she put everything she had into getting the door open.

I joined her a second later, and together we pushed.

The hatch cracked at last, and a soft hue of light filled the ancient stairwell.

14

WE RAN THROUGH THE SNOW, trying to get as far from the hatch as possible. When we were halfway across the white field, the ground shook with so much intensity that I nearly fell to my knees.

Abby caught my arm, helping me to balance. "Keep going!" she yelled through the noise.

Lucia was still on my back, making things even more difficult, but I wouldn't let that stop me.

We trudged through the snow, slowing but never stopping. Finally, as we neared a ridge, I turned to see the stairwell begin to collapse in on itself. The hard snow cracked in every direction, breaking apart like glass before sinking in on itself.

Lucia slapped the side of my head. "Don't stop now, boy!"

I swept my hand over my eyes and nose, wiping the snow away. There was a formation in the snow, leading to a lower area from the ridge. More rocks there than snow, which probably made for a better foundation. "There!" I yelled, pointing. "Come on!"

Abigail followed as I steadily ascended the cliff, minding my footing. If I slipped, I might hurt Lucia, and as tough as she might be for an old woman, I wagered she could do without another injury.

We were halfway down the ridge when I heard the explosion. I turned back to the field to see a cloud of snow burst into the air. *The stairwell must have collapsed*, I thought before proceeding forward again.

I reached the rocks and offered my hand to Abby. She took it, stepping off the edge of the ridge. "Are both of you okay?" she asked.

"We're fine," I said. "But that won't last if we don't find a way out of this storm."

"Can you reach Siggy from here?" Abigail asked.

"I can try," I said, tapping my ear and opening a channel. "Siggy, this is Jace. Respond."

"C...tain...ference...storm..." Sigmond responded, his voice broken and distorted.

"Repeat!" I ordered. "Siggy, you're not coming in clear."

"...ologies...aptain...repeat...static..."

"Godsdammit," I muttered. "I hate this planet."

"You aren't alone in that," said Lucia.

"We'll have to wait this storm out or get closer to the ship," I said.

"Is the signal that weak?" asked Abigail.

"On a clear day with zero interference, my comm can reach two kilometers," I said. "We're drowning in snow and I have no idea where we even are."

"Half a day's walk," said Lucia.

"Right, so not close," I said. I looked at the old woman over my shoulder. "Any ideas?"

"There is one place that I know of, but I'm hesitant," she said.

"If you know somewhere, then tell us," said Abigail.

Lucia paused then let out a brief sigh. She pointed to my right, toward the rising sun. "That way. Look for another ridge."

I took a step, kicking snow from my foot. "Where are you leading us exactly? Not another facility, I hope."

"No, nothing like that," she answered, her voice growing softer as she spoke. "There is a man living nearby. Someone I know."

WE MARCHED through the thickening snow while winds pushed against us. I felt Lucia hugging my back, burying her face in my coat. I could feel the heating pads inside my clothes working to balance my body temperature, but it wasn't enough to completely offset the cold. I couldn't imagine how Lucia must have felt, despite having grown up here.

This planet was hell, an icy mess of a world with actual monsters and a dying land. There was nothing for the living.

Nothing for Lucia or her people. At a certain point, whether it was tomorrow or a hundred years from now, eventually, they would all die, and no one would remember them.

Except for me, I couldn't help but think. I pushed the thought away. There was no time for that, not with two armies after me.

We found the ridge in under an hour. I tried using my comm several times as we walked but only received a few broken responses.

The ridge was ahead of us, but I couldn't see an opening. As we drew closer, I finally spotted a tarp spread out across the rock, rustling in the wind.

"There!" said Lucia, pointing to the tarp. The winds had picked up even more, making it hard for me to hear her voice, despite being so close. "We need to get inside!"

When we arrived, I had to locate the corner of the cloth. It was tied in a knot and took me several tries to undo. I could barely feel my fingers, after all, making things more difficult than they should be.

After managing to squeeze inside, I reached out and retied the knot, securing the tarp.

The cave was filled with supplies. I spotted a fire pit,

just a few meters inside, with some blankets tossed against both walls.

Abigail helped me pull Lucia off my back and place her against the wall. I stretched my arms and shoulders, relieved to have the weight off. "Damn, woman," I said, twisting my torso and popping my spine. "Let's not do that again."

"Who's there?!" called a voice from deeper inside the cave.

I was about to answer, when I saw someone appear from the back, poking their head out from behind another wall. "Hey, don't mind us," I said, folding my arms.

Abigail placed a hand on her weapon. Smart, considering neither of us had ever seen this person before.

"What are you doing here?" asked the stranger. He approached us, holding an object in his hand.

I quickly drew my pistol but didn't aim it. If he tried anything, I wouldn't hesitate to take him out. I didn't care who he was or how Lucia knew him. "Stop right there," I said, brushing my finger over the trigger. "Don't take another step."

The man looked at each of us then at Lucia. I saw the realization wash across his face as he began to understand. "Lucia? I-is that you?"

"It's me, Josef," she said, trying to sit up. "Now would you put that stupid thing away before these two wind up shooting you?"

"Are you hurt? What happened?" he asked, quickly

placing the weapon behind him and shuffling closer to her. "Was it the storm? Did you fall?"

"Boneclaws," she said, fanning him away. "I'm fine. Quit your worrying."

Josef seemed wrought with concern, his eyes darting all over Lucia's body, examining her. "Why are you on the floor if you're fine? Can't you stand?"

"Get off, you old dasick," she snapped.

I looked at Abigail. "What did she just call him?"

"Sounded bad," she said. "It must not translate."

Josef rolled her leg sleeve up, spotting several marks and a large bruise. "That's what I thought," he said, shaking his head. "I'll be back in a moment."

He got to his feet and went to the rear of the cave. I waited until he was far enough away before I said anything to Lucia. "Who the hell is that guy?"

"Josef," she muttered. "My husband."

"Your *what*?" asked Abigail.

Lucia scowled at the nun but kept her mouth shut. Josef came running, bowls in his arms, hurrying to Lucia's side. "I'll get you fixed up right away," he said, taking a wet cloth in one hand and a small, clear pouch in the other.

"What's that?" I asked.

"Huh? Oh, it's just a bit of medical gel," said Josef. He leaned in closer to Lucia. "Who are these people?"

"Lost visitors," I said.

"They're from another world," said Lucia, grabbing the gel package out of his hand. She began to apply it to herself. "I was helping them through the tunnels, when we were attacked."

"Visitors? From space? After all this time, someone's finally come to our little home," said Josef. "I didn't think I'd live long enough to see it."

"That seems like the common reaction around here," I said. "Say, Jo, you think we could stay here for a bit? I can't contact my people in this storm."

"Of course!" he exclaimed, more enthusiastically than I'd expected. "Please, friends, have a seat. Make yourselves comfortable. I have some meals if you'd like."

I imagined what sort of food someone living in a cave might have, but figured it couldn't be too bad if he was still alive.

"No, thank you," said Abigail, who seemed to have come to a different conclusion.

"Please, you have to eat something," said Josef. He snapped to his feet and went to the corner, not far from the fire pit.

Abigail looked at me. "If he brings me a plate of Boneclaw meat, I'll throw it at you."

"Boneclaw?" Lucia asked, scoffing. "What sort of food do you think we eat?"

"Give it a chance," I said. "I'll eat a little Boneclaw if it means surviving."

"You just ate this morning. You can't go one night without food?" Abby asked.

"And risk the hunger pain setting in? No, thanks," I said.

Josef returned, holding several thin boxes. "Ration meals. I'll have them heated and ready to eat soon, if you want them."

He handed me a box, and I folded the top up, checking it. The meal was covered by a plastic material, all of the food vacuum-sealed. Vegetables, meat, gravy. "Where did you get this?" I finally asked.

"Janus has a machine that recycles material and creates food," said Lucia. "We have to return as much of the materials as we can in order to continue to create new food."

"This is recycled?" asked Abigail.

"Abby, let it go," I said, handing the box to Josef. "We'll have that meal, pal."

Josef smiled warmly. "Wonderful!"

THE WIND outside the cave howled as we sat together near the fire pit. Josef had cooked each of the boxed meals and handed them back to us. I peeled the plastic back and let the steam rise from inside. I couldn't help but think that this wasn't how you were supposed to make these, but said nothing.

With a shrug, I dug in.

The food was a little bland, but better than nothing. I

glanced at Abigail, who ate her food without complaint, which meant it couldn't be that bad.

Josef took our empty boxes when we were done and walked to the rear of the cave. Abigail decided this would be a good time to bug Lucia about her connection to this weird cave-person. I really didn't give two shits about any of it. If Lucia wanted to have a secret husband who lived in a cave and ate out of boxes, that was her business.

"It's complicated," Lucia told the nun.

"How?" asked Abby. "Did he get banished from your tribe?"

Lucia scoffed. "Don't be ridiculous. He's here because he wants to be."

"What? Why would he want to be here?" Abigail asked.

"Because he's a selfish old fool," said Lucia.

"Hey, Jo," I called, my voice echoing through the cave. "Abby wants to know why you're here."

Abigail smacked my arm. "Jace, you're not supposed to—"

"What?" I asked with a shrug. "This way, you can go straight to the source and bypass all this annoying drama."

Lucia opened her mouth to say something, no doubt a string of insults directed at me, but was cut off by Josef's response. "Oh? Didn't anyone back home tell you about my work?" he asked, returning quickly. "I'm living here because I'm looking for Tritium cores."

I paused at the term. Was this guy serious? Had Lucia somehow found a way to tell him about the core in my pack? I'd only just found the damn thing. "What did you just say?"

"Tritium cores," he repeated. "They're used for vital systems throughout the old buildings, but there is only one for each structure. The one we use for our village has begun to lose its power, mostly due to the animals burrowing through the—"

"You mean the Boneclaws?" Abigail asked.

"That's right," said Josef. "The Boneclaws move constantly, nesting in different areas, digging new tunnels all the time. They've broken many systems in the process."

"We've seen the tunnels," she said. "Have you managed to find any of these cores on your own?"

Josef frowned. "No, the herbology facility's core seems to be unreachable. I've searched every conceivable—"

I shot a glance at Abigail. She stared back at me, her eyes falling on the bag tied to my waist. "Jace…" she whispered to me, but I only shook my head.

"What's wrong?" asked Josef.

"Could you please excuse us for a moment," said Abigail, getting on her feet. She motioned for me to follow, but I only stared at her. "Jace, can I have a word with you?"

I sighed. "Fine."

We walked to the back of the cave, leaving the married couple alone to presumably squabble.

When we were out of earshot, Abigail leaned closer to me. "We have to give them that core," she whispered.

"I don't know what you're talking about," I said.

"Don't be like that, Jace. I saw it in your hand when you came out of the tunnel," she said.

"Then you know it's too valuable to hand off to a homeless person in a cave," I answered.

Abby shrugged. "Maybe, but we should at least talk to Karin and Lucia about this."

"What happens if *Titan* picks us up and needs this sometime down the line?" I asked. "We've already seen what happens when a core runs out of juice."

"I know," she said simply. "But it isn't ours to take."

"You had no problem stealing one from the Union," I said.

"You know that's different. These people are our friends. They've helped us at every turn."

I groaned. "Okay, okay. I hear what you're saying," I said. "We'll hand it over, but not until we get back in their camp and verify all this with the rest of the team."

"Deal," said Abby, smiling at her little victory.

"Fine, but there's no need to be so smug about it," I said with some sarcasm in my voice, although she knew I didn't mean it.

She laughed, leaning in and kissing my cheek. "Let's stay the night and head out in the morning."

My face warmed the way it did after a few shots of whiskey. Abigail smiled and walked past me, joining the others near the front of the cave.

I just stood there like a fool, wondering what the hell was wrong with me.

15

THE HOTEL ROOM smelled like strawberries, expensive booze, and perfume, and the orange glow of the city crept in through the drapes. It was the middle of the night and it was time for me to go.

I sat up in bed, pulling away from the naked woman beside me. From Eliza.

She stirred, waking to see me right as I was getting to my feet. "Time to go?" she asked.

"Yeah. Go back to sleep," I told her. "I'll see you when I get back."

"Sure, when you get back," she mumbled right before she drifted back into whatever dream she was having.

I threw on my shirt and buttoned my pants, then left the room key on the counter. Eliza would handle the bill. She always did whenever we had these little meetups.

I'd been in this business for four years, working on glorified errands for Eliza and her bosses. Not that I minded the jobs, but they were only a stepping stone to something greater. Something involving me, cruising the galaxy in my own ship, free to live the life I wanted.

Fuck everyone else.

In the meantime, this job was getting me there, and fast. I'd already made contacts through the network, learned how the Renegade business went. I couldn't just get a ship and fly off on my own, not without knowing the right people beforehand. I had to learn who the good agents were—the people handing out jobs and managing information. Without a good agent, you couldn't make it very far in this business. I'd already met a few of them, including Marta Sosen and some dopey-looking jerk on Taurus Station (Ollie, I think his name was), but I wanted at least four contacts before I got my feet wet.

Which was what I was doing right now, heading out to meet a guy named Genji Marco in a bar across town.

I'd met Genji on a job back in Sandis, a crappy little town on the other side of the planet. We were there to pay someone else a visit, break a few bones if we had to, but it never came to that. We mostly spent the weekend sitting in a parking lot, waiting for the target to show. That was when Genji told me about Fratley Oxanos, some loan shark with money to spare. The man who could give me a ship. It was exactly the sort of contact I needed to finally get on with my life.

Walking through the Grand Deluxe's lobby, I noticed an empty street ahead, probably due to the recent drop in temperature. It was freezing in the city this time of year. It might even be snowing when I returned from my next assignment.

I clutched the coat I was wearing and called a nearby cab to pick me up.

"HUGHES!" exclaimed Genji as I entered the Torchlight Bar. He was sitting at a side table, nearly done with what I could only assume wasn't his first beer.

"Genji," I said with a nod.

He gave me a cheeky smile. "Been a while, you glorious bastard."

I took a seat at his table and signaled the waitress. "Another two of these."

Genji sat across from me, smacking both his knees. "Boy, it's good to see you. I gotta say, half the crews I've worked with haven't been as fun as ours."

I nodded. "Tell me about it."

The waitress brought us another round a few moments later, and we caught up on what we'd been up to in the six months since the last time we'd seen each other.

"Tell me about this girl you're seeing," he said.

"She's nobody," I muttered, taking another sip of beer. I wiped my mouth on my sleeve.

"Nobody?" he asked. "Ain't you ready to settle down?"

"Me?" I scoffed. "No, thanks. Besides, Eliza isn't interested in a relationship."

"How's that?" he asked.

I shrugged. "We just get together when I'm in town. It's nothing serious."

I wasn't lying. Eliza had told me, back when we started our relationship, that it would never amount to more than a fling. She called it an "arrangement." Something to keep us occupied and satisfied. I couldn't say it bothered me, because it really didn't. Even if she offered me a place in upper management, I'd never give up my dream of being a Renegade. Not for her or anyone else in this damn galaxy.

"Well, you're a lucky S-O-B, Jace. Ain't every day you find a woman willing to bed you and not ask for much else," said Genji.

"Maybe if you were prettier, the ladies would pay more attention," I said with a light shrug.

He frowned. "Damn, man, that's cold. You know how to wound a fella."

We ordered another round and shared a laugh. It was nice to talk with a friend. Being with Eliza was fine, the way I saw it, but she barely spoke a word most nights. She had one thing on her mind, same as me, and once it was done, we had little else to discuss.

"So I suppose we ought to get to why we're here, eh?" asked Genji. "You wanna know about old Fratley."

"You mentioned he could get me a ship," I said.

Genji nodded. "He's got a scrapyard full of them. Sells them at a discount. He even offers loans if you ain't got the money."

"Sounds perfect," I said.

"Yeah, but you need a few thousand for the trip," he said. "Think you can round that up?"

"A few thousand?" I asked, a little surprised. "He's not on Bordo?"

"Nah, he and his Ravagers live out in the middle of nowhere. It's five tunnels from here," explained Genji.

Five slip tunnels meant at least two days' travel, so the high cost made sense, but I hadn't planned for this. "When you told me about this guy, I thought he was here. I've only got 7800 credits to my name, Genji."

"That's more than enough for the trip," he said.

"But it's not even close to what I'd need to buy a ship from him, is it?" I asked.

He paused, thinking about it. "Yeah," he said, slowly nodding. "Yeah, you got a point. But hey, what if you use the rest as a down payment?"

"Would that work?" I asked.

He shrugged. "Sure, I've seen guys do it all the time."

"I don't know, Genji. Is taking a loan from this guy a smart idea?" I asked.

My current job revolved around getting other people to pay what they owed. I knew how this game was played. The last thing I needed was a broken arm because I couldn't fork over my payments.

Genji waved a hand at me. "Don't worry about that, Jace. Fratley's an ex-Renegade. He can probably offer you a few jobs to get you started."

"He used to be a Renegade?" I asked, intrigued.

Genji nodded. "One of the best, from what I hear. Now look at him. The man is swimming in creds. That could be *you*, Jace. Think about it."

My eyes dropped to the table while Genji took another drink. I'd spent most of my life looking for an opportunity like this. Every action had taken me a step closer to this moment. All I had to do was reach out and take what I wanted, but it would mean taking a huge risk and betting on a man I'd never met.

But wasn't that the way the universe worked? You placed a bet on the odds, based on what you wanted, and hoped for the best. I was twenty-eight years old. If I stayed on Boson, I'd eventually save enough money to get my own ship, maybe become a Renegade when I was forty.

To hell with that.

I knew what I wanted. I knew what it took to get there. If Genji was right and this Fratley person could really help me, why shouldn't I seize the opportunity?

"How long?" I finally asked, a serious look on my face. I leaned forward, staring my friend in the eye. "How long do I have before we can go?"

He set the glass down and smiled. "I'm only here until tomorrow. Then I'm gone."

I hesitated. That really didn't give me much time.

"Is that enough for you?" he asked. "I'll be back this way in six months if you want to sit on it."

I slowly shook my head. "No...No, I can't wait that long."

"What about your lady friend? Won't she miss you if you take off to another star system?"

"Eliza doesn't give two shits if I leave tomorrow or six months from now. She'll find someone else in a week." I turned away, looking at the door. "Besides, this is what matters."

He smiled. "That's the Jace I know! No one can ever hold you down." He raised his glass. "Here's to getting what you really want in life! Cheers!"

"Cheers," I echoed, and together we dinked our glasses.

16

I OPENED my eyes in the cave, and the first thing I saw was Abigail's hair against my chest. She was fast asleep, breathing steadily.

I wiped the grime from my eyes, then eased myself out from under Abigail. She shifted but didn't wake.

Lucia and Josef were lying together on the other side of the fire pit, wrapped beneath a blanket. I didn't want to imagine what the two of them had gotten into while Abby and I had been asleep.

Without waking anyone, I got to my feet and put on my coat, then took one of the nearby blankets and wrapped it around myself. The tarp was lightly tossing as I rolled it up and stepped outside into the cold. The snow had finally stopped falling, but it was still freezing.

The blue and yellow sky was so bright that it made me

squint, letting my eyes adjust to the new day. The sun was barely above the horizon, but I felt like I'd slept for days.

I tapped my ear, activating the comm. "Siggy, it's me. Can you hear me?"

"Hello, Captain Hughes," returned Sigmond.

I breathed a sigh of relief at the sound of his voice. "Finally. Listen, pal. I need a pickup. Think you can track my signal?"

"Of course, sir," answered the A.I. "May I ask how your visit has been treating you?"

"Not too great," I said, unzipping my pants. "I'm in a cave in the middle of nowhere, pissing in the snow. I'm ready to get the hell out of here."

"Very understandable, sir," said Sigmond. "Location verified. Shall I bring the ship to your current location?"

"Yeah, but send a message to Freddie and Dressler. Tell them you're giving us a lift back to town," I said.

"Understood, sir," said Sigmond. "Stand by for pick up."

I relaxed at last, staring off into the long stretch of white before me.

"Nice day, eh?" asked a voice behind me.

I flinched, surprised, but still pissing in the snow. "What the—"

Josef chuckled. "Oh, I'm sorry," he said, letting out a light chuckle. "I didn't mean to interrupt."

"What are you doing out here?" I asked, trying to hurry up.

"I was just checking on you," he said. "But I see now that you're okay."

I zipped up my pants. "I'm fine, and ready to leave in just a few minutes. My ship's coming to get us."

"That's great news!" exclaimed Josef. "You'll have to visit me again sometime soon, if it's convenient. I spend most of my time alone out here, and let me tell you, it gets to be a little boring."

"Why is that exactly?" I asked. "You said that Tritium core was important. Why don't the others help you?"

He frowned. "They tried, bless them, but we lost a few too many people. I'm the only one who wanted to keep looking. It's dangerous, but if we can locate a new core, it will change everything."

"How? The village seemed fine to me. How much better can a new power source make it?" I asked.

"It sounds like you didn't see everything. There are several systems that have stopped working over the last one hundred years. The younger generation thinks they can manage without them, but I remember how life used to be." He shook his head. "We had a transport vessel that could take us anywhere within two hundred kilometers. Did they tell you about that?"

"Can't say they did," I said.

"It has a rechargeable battery," he explained. "Once the core broke, we decided not to waste the energy on it. Not that it matters too much, since there's nowhere to go on this planet, but it made scavenging easier. We were able to extend our reach and carry more supplies from the other facilities. Since then, we've dwindled and lost so much. It pains my heart to imagine the future. My grandchildren's quality of life will have diminished so much compared to my father's father. That isn't progress." He took a slow breath. "It's a slow death."

I was impressed by the old codger's resourcefulness. It took a certain kind of person to survive on their own in the middle of nowhere, surrounded by a wasteland. For him to willingly do that in order to search for a core that might or might not exist was something else. Maybe the rest of his people didn't believe in him—though, I was pretty sure Lucia did, despite her anger—but Abigail and I knew the truth. We knew he was right.

"You really think a core would help your people that much?" I asked, staring at him.

"I do," he said simply, and I knew from the look on his face that it was true.

"In that case, you should come back with us to the village. We could use your help with something," I suggested.

"Help?" he asked.

"I need to talk to Karin about it, but I might have a solution for your problem. There might not be a reason for you to stay out here," I said. "When we get back to the village, stay with your wife and don't go anywhere."

"What do you mean?" he asked. "What can you do?"

"Trust me," I said. "If everything works out, you may not have to come back to this cave ever again."

Josef said nothing as I turned toward the cave. He only followed me inside, no doubt thinking about what I had told him. No doubt he was probably wondering what I'd meant by all of that. I didn't take him for a fool, given how resourceful he'd been to live like this, but I couldn't tell him about the core just yet. Not until I spoke with Karin and made sure these people knew how to handle something as powerful as a Tritium Core. All without blowing themselves to Hell and back.

I opened the tarp to see Abigail sitting beside Lucia, talking quietly. "Glad to see you're awake," I said.

She beamed a smile at me. "You're not as smooth as you think, sneaking out of here."

"Your wife was just telling me about her childhood home," said Lucia.

I cringed at the term. "She's not my wife."

"Oh? Could've fooled me," said the old woman.

I scoffed. "You're one to talk, all snuggled up with Jo here."

Josef walked past me. "Well, in our case, she actually is my wife," he said, grinning.

"For now," said Lucia, scowling at him.

He frowned. "I thought you forgave me last night."

"I'll forgive you when you stop living in this cave," she said flatly.

After successfully diverting the conversation, I motioned at Abigail, hoping to get a word in before the four of us left.

"Everything okay, Jace?" she asked when she was closer.

"I just wanted to make sure you still have our little prize," I said.

"If you mean the core, it's in my bag," she whispered, opening up her pouch in front of me. I spotted the object immediately, nestled between two pieces of cloth. She covered it and tied the top of the bag. "Don't worry."

I nodded. "Good. Don't let that thing out of your sight. Not until we talk to Karin and verify everything Jo told us."

"What's that about Karin?" asked Lucia.

I cursed myself for talking too loudly. "Nothing. We just need to meet with her when we get back. There's a lot to talk about."

"If you're worried about the transmission, don't be," said Lucia. "If I know my daughter, she's taken care of it by now."

I decided it would probably be a good idea to change the subject. "Say, Jo, when was the last time you saw Karin? She's your kid, right?"

Josef smiled. "Oh, yes, isn't she wonderful? I haven't seen her in a few weeks. How is she doing, Lucia?"

"She'd be better with her father around," said the old woman.

Josef frowned again. "Oh, Lucia, please don't be upset with me."

"That was easy," I muttered.

THE FOUR OF us left the cave and headed west, trudging slowly through the snow. Josef knew the way to the field where Siggy could land the ship. He guided our path through a piece of land where the snow seemed thinner and the walk was easier.

Josef and I carried Lucia between us on a bed matt, while Abby kept watch with her weapon ready. According to the old man, animals often emerged from their hiding places the day after a harsh storm, which meant there was a good chance we might run into something that hadn't eaten in days.

"Siggy, what's your status?" I asked once we'd reached the clearing.

"Apologies, Captain, but Dr. Dressler and Frederick insisted I wait for them."

"I didn't authorize that, Sigmond," I snapped, not hiding my annoyance. "You're supposed to be here already."

"Sorry about that, Captain!" Freddie blurted out, a frantic tone in his voice.

"Godsdammit, Freddie. Just get over here! We're stuck in the fucking snow!"

"S-sorry, sir! On our way!"

Abigail was staring at me, listening in on her own comm. "I guess that means we'll have to wait here for a few more minutes."

I clenched my teeth. "It's fine. It will take them five minutes to get here, worst case. I can stand the cold for that long. I just don't like it very much."

A loud cry rang out, echoing through the valley.

We all froze, Abigail and I looking at each other. "What was that?" she asked.

Another scream, louder than the last, coming from across the valley. Maybe closer. It was hard to tell.

"Oh, no," muttered Josef, taking a step back. He raised a finger, pointing to the nearby ridge, overlooking the valley.

I looked but couldn't see it clearly. A ball of white, large, and standing on the mound of white snow. It raised its claws, slamming them down on the snow, and then roared again. I reached for my rifle quickly and checked my ammunition. "Fuck," I blurted out. I was nearly empty, with only a handful of shots left in the magazine. "Abby, how's your—"

"I've got half a mag," she said before I could even finish the sentence.

I'd already examined my pistol back in the cave. I knew I still had twelve bullets, ready and waiting, between the two handguns. "Josef, buddy, you got any tricks in your bag?" I asked, glancing sideways at the old man.

He retrieved the weapon he'd first pulled on us when we found him. "Only this, but it isn't much," he admitted.

The monster roared again and beat its fists. It leapt forward, gliding down the slope and into the valley.

"Fire!" I barked, and fired the last remaining bullets in my rifle.

The animal took it all. It kicked snow and flailed its massive arms, finally bolting toward us. I felt my chest tighten with anticipation, watching as death itself set me in its path.

Abigail's shots collided with the Boneclaw, right as it was getting close. As all our firepower converged, the creature toppled over, losing its footing in the thick snow.

The monster fumbled a few meters but kept kicking towards us, trying to push itself back up.

Jo grabbed his wife and dragged her out of the fray. Any longer and the animal would have found her there, ripe for the killing.

"I'm out!" screamed Abigail, just before the Boneclaw managed to get back to its feet. It had taken a bad spill but wouldn't be deterred for long. Several bullet holes marked its white body, little bits of blood oozing from its wounds. The creature took all of this in stride, determined to get its kills.

I tossed my rifle in the snow, the magazine finally empty, and retrieved my pistols.

I rapidly fired each gun, hitting the animal multiple times in the chest, but it barely slowed. It tilted its head, its blind face filled with a vacant expression. As I cocked the pistol, the creature's ears twitched, and it replied with a sharp yelp, turning its head back, like it was calling for someone.

I fired three quick shots, hitting its shoulder and neck. The monster snapped toward me and roared, showing its many teeth.

"Aim for the eyes!" screamed Josef. His voice sounded far away, even though he was right there.

I pulled the pistol around so I was looking down the barrel.

I would only have one chance to land this shot.

As the Boneclaw charged toward me, I held my breath.

The bullet hit the target, piercing the beast's skull and coming out the other side, pulling brains and blood with it.

The Boneclaw collapsed instantly.

I didn't believe it at first. We'd filled this thing with so many shots by now that I couldn't be certain of anything. I just stood there, staring at the body, breathing mist into the air, unable to speak. I kept thinking it was about to get back up at any moment.

But the animal never moved.

I swallowed, slowly lowering my gun. "Is everyone okay?" I asked, looking at Abigail.

She said nothing, but I could hear Josef laughing behind me. "You did it!" he exclaimed. "Oh, thank the ancestors!"

Abigail walked closer to the dead animal, slowly, and bent to look at its face. "Nice shot."

"Or lucky," I said, holstering both pistols.

She stood. "Either way, it was still nice."

A sudden roar erupted through the valley. Both of us turned, back on guard again.

The first cry was followed by another, leading our eyes to the same cliff we had spotted the last Boneclaw.

There, no different from the first, stood another. It raised its claws into the sky, screaming out into the valley.

"No!" snapped Abigail. "Not another one!"

"Not just one," said Josef. "Look!"

Two more poked their heads above the ridgeline, joining the first. Each of them stood in a line, beside one another, watching us as we retrieved our guns, next to their fallen kin.

I tapped my ear, activating the comm. "Freddie, gods-dammit!" I barked. "Where the hell are you?! We're about to be overrun! Get your asses over here!"

The animals dropped from the cliff, coming down the slope, charging all at once. "What are we going to do?!" screamed Josef.

I cocked my pistol, taking aim at the first of the pack. I was pretty sure we couldn't handle three of these things, not without more firepower.

But before I could do or say anything else, I felt the low hum of an engine, burning in the sky.

A missile slammed into the snow beneath the first Boneclaw, blowing its legs clean out from under it. Blood went everywhere, settling like dust.

The *Renegade Star* fired armor-piercing rounds, along

with another two missiles, filling the other Boneclaws with enough firepower to take out a small tank.

They died instantly.

"I apologize for the delay, sir," said Sigmond, his voice filling my ear. "I do hope we weren't too late."

"Siggy, you sneaky bastard!" I yelled, like it was my birthday.

"Captain!" exclaimed Freddie, waving from the cockpit window. "Sorry we're late! Is everyone okay down there?"

I looked at Abigail to see her staring at the fresh Boneclaw corpses...or what was left of them anyway. "Pretty sure we're all right. Why don't you set her down so we can head out?"

"Understood, sir," said Sigmond.

I glanced back at Josef and Lucia, who were both staring slack-jawed at the *Star*. "Hey, you two okay?" I asked.

"I-is that a ship?" asked Josef, pointing a shaking finger and refusing to take his eyes off of it.

"It sure as hell is," I said, cracking a smirk. "A damn fine ship."

17

WE LAID Lucia on the couch in the lounge, telling Josef to stay with her while the rest of us took to the upper deck of the cargo bay.

"Thanks for the pickup, even though you were so late, you nearly got us all killed," I said once the four of us were inside and the door was shut. I narrowed my eyes at Freddie, who looked so guilty, you'd swear he just killed his own mother. "There's things that need discussing. One, in particular."

Dressler stood with her arms behind her, regarding me. "What is it? Did something happen while you were out there? Does it have anything to do with that strange old man?"

"We found something that he's been looking for," I said. "Abby?"

Abigail nodded, reaching into her pack and pulling out the Tritium core, showing it to the others.

Dressler's eyes widened. "Where did you find that?"

"Underground, beneath a giant plant monster," I said.

Freddie and Dressler gave me a confused look.

"Don't ask," I said. "Point is, I'm pretty sure it still works."

"Fascinating," muttered Dressler, touching the glass on the container. "To think, something like this was buried under a mountain of snow."

"We're thinking of giving it back to Karin and her people," said Abby.

"Giving it back?" asked Freddie. "But do they even understand how to use something like this?"

"That's the question I want to ask before we hand it over," I said. "Josef has been out here, trying to find one of these for years. The way he tells it, the old one is dying. Not sure how long it's got before it finally gives, but they've been shutting systems down one-by-one to conserve energy."

"I see," said Dressler, nodding slowly. "So this core will fix quite a few of their problems."

"That's the idea," I said.

The doctor stared at the device for a moment. "Then if that's the case, Captain, you should do it," she said, looking up at me.

"You think I should hand it over?" I asked.

"If it helps them survive," she said.

I looked at Abigail then back at Dressler. "I gotta say, Doc, I'm surprised you're okay with that."

"Why? Do you think because I'm associated with the Union, I don't know how to empathize with other people?" she asked.

I chuckled. "It's not that. I just figured you'd be worried about them getting their hands on what could amount to a weapon of mass destruction."

She nodded. "There is that, of course, but technology itself is neither good nor evil. It comes down to the person wielding it and what their intentions are," explained Dressler. "And from what I've seen of Karin and the others, there is no ill-intent in this place. Only a will to survive."

"Besides, they've been living with the other core for two thousand years," said Freddie.

"Right," said Dressler. "If they wanted to hurt themselves, they would have done so by now."

I felt the ship tilt, turning as we made our final approach to the other landing site. "We have arrived, sir," Siggy told me. "Please prepare to disembark."

"Looks like we're here," I told the others.

Abby stuffed the Tritium core back in her bag. "Always on the move."

Freddie opened the door and stepped out, followed by Abigail.

Dressler hesitated behind them, thumbing her wrist and staring at the dash.

"Something wrong?" I asked her, pausing at the door.

"You're really going to hand over something so valuable to a group of people you barely know?" she asked.

I smirked. "I know. It's stupid, isn't it?"

"Stupid?"

"If this were a year ago, I would've stolen that thing and sold it, no questions asked."

"And now?" she asked.

I shrugged. "I guess I just figure they need it more than we do. What's with all the questions, Doc?"

"Nothing," she said, quickly sliding past me. "Let's just get going."

―――――――

WHILE ABIGAIL and I had been out in the middle of nowhere, stuck in a storm, the others had gone through the trouble of establishing a stable communications system between the *Renegade Star* and the underground city. The repeaters were fully operational, it seemed, and I could easily contact Karin and Janus whenever I felt like it.

"We have a team ready to escort you back," said Karin, her voice coming through the comm.

"That'd be just fine," I said, standing with everyone in the lounge, ready to disembark.

"They'll be waiting for you near the cave," she said.

I walked over to the coffee maker and poured myself a fresh cup. "See you soon, then."

The comm clicked off right as I went to take a sip of the brew. "Ah," I said. "Tastes like shit."

"Why do you keep drinking that if you hate it so much?" asked Dressler.

"You take what you can get," I said with a shrug.

Freddie leaned closer to Dressler. "The captain used to have a better machine, but it was broken. We pulled this from a Union ship."

"You stole that thing?" she asked.

"W-well," stuttered Freddie. "It was complicated."

"They tried to kidnap me and Lex," said Abigail.

"And murder the rest of us," I said. "Ask Alphonse about all that the next time you see him."

"Why?" she asked.

I set the half-empty cup on the counter and walked to the nearby hall, ready to leave. "He was part of their crew."

We grabbed our gear and left through the cargo bay, entering the white field and heading back to the city. It took no time at all to find our way through the tunnels, given how many times we'd made this trip by now as well as the armed guards at our side.

When the door to the inner sanctum opened, I saw Karin standing there, waiting. She smiled when she saw us, but her expression changed the moment Lucia appeared, being carried between two soldiers.

"Mother!" she exclaimed, rushing to the old woman's side.

"She took a hit, but she'll be okay," said Abigail.

Karin was about to say something else, when she saw Josef enter behind the guards. "F-father?" she said.

The old man smiled, extending his arms to give her a hug. She ran into him, and he pulled her close. "Karin!" he said, pressing his cheek to her hair.

"What are you doing here?" she asked. "I thought you were doing your research."

"I was, but your new friends stopped by to pay me a visit, along with your mother," he answered, beaming.

"Your dad really helped us out," I said, giving Josef a slight nod. "That storm left us with nowhere to go. We might have died if he hadn't been living in that shithole of a cave."

"What an odd way to compliment someone," observed Dressler.

"I do what I can," I said, fanning my hand at her.

Abigail touched Karin's shoulder. "We need to talk to you about something. Can you spare a minute?"

"Of course," she answered, looking curious. "What's the matter?"

"Not here, please," said the nun.

Karin nodded. "The council room, then," she suggested.

"The one Janus took us to?" I asked.

She nodded. "Shall I invite him as well?"

"Sure," I said. "He should probably hear about this anyway."

"What about Lucia?" asked Freddie.

"I'll be fine," said the old woman. "Take care of your business. Josef and I will be in the medical center. I'll take a nap in the pod and be good as new in a few hours."

"You have a medical pod?" asked Abigail.

"Two of them, actually," said Karin.

I cocked my eye in surprise. "You didn't tell us about that. What other tech do you have stashed away in this place?"

"Wouldn't you like to know," said Lucia, chuckling like a crazy person as the two soldiers carried her away.

WE SAT around the table in the conference room as Janus appeared, materializing out of thin air. Before any of us could say a word, he looked directly at Abigail. "Is that what I think it is?"

Abigail opened her mouth but paused. "What do you mean?" she finally asked.

"The object in your bag," he said.

"You know what's in there?" I asked.

He nodded. "The emitters in this room can detect certain devices, types of metal, and energy emissions. In this case, the presence of the core has set off an internal alarm."

"An alarm?" asked Freddie.

"It's probably because of how dangerous it is," suggested Dressler.

"Precisely so," said Janus. "May I ask you, Captain, where did you find such a device? Further, why have you brought it into this facility?"

Karin looked at me. "What is he talking about?"

I gave Abigail a nod to let her know it was time. She took the Tritium core from her bag and set it on the table. "We found it in the other facility," she explained.

"That's a Tritium core?" asked Karin, blinking at the device like she'd never seen anything like it. "M-my father was right! There really was another one out there!"

"He was," I said. "We found it near the area he was already looking. This just happened to be buried under a pit filled with man-eating plants."

She eyed the core, leaning across the table. "Amazing," she muttered, like she'd never seen one before.

"Don't you have one of these?" I asked.

"Yes, but I've never been near it in person," she said.

"The core sits behind three layers of protective casing. Due to its instability, I've prohibited anyone from going near it," said Janus.

"It can't be moved?" I asked.

He shook his head. "It can, but only with great care. Given the lack of a viable replacement, there was simply no need to take such a risk. The core was still operational, albeit to a limited extent, so we decided to leave it where it sat until another one could be located."

"Looks like today is your lucky day, then," I said.

Karin's eyes widened at that. "Are you giving this to us?"

"Only if you can show you understand it," I answered.

"How do you mean?" she asked.

"Jace wants to make sure you aren't going to blow yourselves up with it," said Abigail.

Dressler cleared her throat. "A necessary concern, all things considered."

"Once the new core is inserted, the lockdown protocol will take effect," said Janus. "Systems will resume full operations and prevent anyone from ever interfering with it again."

"Once you get it working, what happens?" asked Freddie.

"Power will be fully restored," said Janus.

"But what does that mean?" he asked. "What other systems will come online?"

"Over the last five hundred years, roughly eighty-seven subsystems have lost functionality," said the Cognitive. "Those include several food synthesizers, additional medical bays, global satellite uplinks, short and long-range transport vessels, and defense."

"What was that about defense?" I asked.

Janus waved his hand and the wall changed to show several images. Several were from the surface. "This planet was originally armed with six ground-to-space missile platforms, only two of which are connected to this facility.

Besides those, we also have two satellites in orbit with defensive capabilities."

"You mean you could blow a ship up from the ground if you wanted?" asked Abigail.

"Indeed," said Janus. "Although that would only happen if there was an impending threat."

"Like the people you told us about," said Karin.

This changed things. If I gave these people this core, they'd have the ability to blow my ship right out of the sky. At the same time, it would give them a fighting chance, should the Union ever find them.

"Why didn't we see the satellites when we entered the system?" asked Freddie.

"They could have crashed by now," explained Janus. "In fact, that scenario is the most likely. Two thousand years is a long time for a satellite to remain in orbit. The decay process may have already set in, depending on a number of factors."

Satellites or not, the land-based missiles were something to consider.

I got to my feet and looked at Abigail. "We need to talk outside," I told her.

Abby nodded, getting up. "Excuse us."

Karin nodded, along with Janus. "Of course. I understand," she said.

Abigail followed me into the hall. "Where are we going?"

"This way," I said, continuing into the other room and making my way to the exit.

The guard saw me coming and took the door handle, turning it. "Headed out?" he asked.

"Just for a second. We'll knock when we need back in," I said.

He nodded and stepped aside.

Abigail and I stepped into the hall, walking a short distance from the entrance. The ancient tunnel had a few artificial lights scattered throughout, illuminating the walls with a gentle ambience.

I leaned against the railing, crossing my arms and looking at Abby. "What do you think?" I asked.

"We don't really have a choice at this point," she said, tapping her chin. "They could take it whenever they want. What could we do to stop them?"

"Good point," I conceded.

"But if they wanted to kill us or take the ship, they would have done it already."

"For a bunch of folks with zero exposure to other cultures, they sure have a talent for diplomacy," I said.

"Maybe that's precisely *why* they're so diplomatic," she countered.

"Fair enough."

"There's also the Union to think about," she added. "If they find this place, they'll wipe it clean. If we walked away from this, we'd be giving Brigham the grand prize."

"Nah," I said, dismissing the notion. "We both know Lex is the prize."

"Second place, then," she said, smiling a little.

We were both quiet for a moment, the weight of everything sinking in. We'd done so much over the last few days on this planet, it was easy to forget what was truly at stake. "Alright," I said finally. "We'll do it, if you think it's the right call."

"Who knows if it is?" she asked, smirking at me. "But sometimes you just have to take a chance on people." She leaned toward me.

I heard a sudden click. "Sir, pardon the interruption," said Sigmond.

I pulled away from Abby and touched my ear. "What is it?"

"I'm detecting a slipspace tear forming on the edge of the star system," he explained. "The same rupture we arrived from."

I shot a hard look at Abigail. She touched her own comm. "Sigmond, who is it? Can you get a clear reading?"

"If my scans are correct, a Union ship," he said, pausing only a second. "Confirmed. The incoming vessel is identified as the *Galactic Dawn.*"

18

ABIGAIL and I raced back to the conference room in a mad panic. "We have to go!" I snapped the second I saw Freddie and Dressler.

"Is something wrong?" asked Janus.

"There's a Union carrier vessel entering this system," I explained.

"They're the people we told you about," said Abigail.

Karin's eyes widened. "The people who have been chasing you?"

I nodded. "The very same. If we don't get out of here, they'll wipe out this entire facility and us along with it."

"What about the core?" asked Dressler.

"We agreed you can use it," said Abigail, looking at Karin. She handed the bag over to her.

"I suggest you get that thing installed as soon as you can and get those guns online," I said.

Karin took the core out of the bag and looked at Janus. "We should go."

"The emitters are down. I won't be able to guide you once you're down there," said the Cognitive.

Dressler stepped closer. "I might be able to help. I've handled one of those before."

"That's not the same as installing one," I said.

"Maybe not, but it's more than anyone else has done," she said. "What other choice do we have?"

"Josef," said Freddie. "Didn't you say he'd spent the last few years studying those things?"

"Hey, that's right," said Abigail.

Freddie smiled. "If he knows how they work, he probably understands how to install one."

"Where is he?" asked Dressler.

I looked at Karin. "Medical?"

She nodded. "Follow me."

JOSEF WAS SITTING beside the pod with Lucia inside. She was sleeping while the machine proceeded to make repairs to her body.

The old man perked up when he saw us, a smile on his face. "Ah, how did the meeting go?"

"We need you to help us replace the old Tritium core with a new one, old man," I said, marching up to him.

He eyed me curiously, his mouth hanging slightly open. "D-did you say you have a Tritium core?"

"I did," I answered. "I picked one up before we met and now we need to use it. Can you help?"

"Is this what you were talking about before, out in the snow when you said you could help us?" he asked.

I nodded. "And right now, there's a ship headed our way. We need to get the defense system online before it gets here."

He looked at Karin, who was standing right behind me. "Is this true?"

He took a step closer to him. "It is. I'm sorry, Father. I know you don't want to leave her right now, but—"

"No, I understand," he said. "We can't risk the lives of our people. I'm ready to go. Just…wait a moment."

I nodded, stepping away from the two of them, back with Abby and the others.

"I have to hurry, but look after your mother for me, Karin," he said, giving his daughter a gentle kiss on the cheek.

"Don't worry, Father. We'll take care of her."

"Good girl," he said, smiling. Josef turned to his wife, looking at her sleeping face through the glass of the pod. "Rest easy, my love."

His eyes lingered on the warrior woman inside for a

long moment, and then, without another word, he turned and walked away.

"But, Captain!" pleaded Freddie.

"Do as I say, Fred," I ordered. "Someone has to be in the ship in case we need an extra set of guns. That someone is *you*."

"What if you need me in the caves?" he asked.

"I've got Abigail and a team of well-trained soldiers. I'll be fine. Your job is more important. That carrier might send its fighters down here, which means you and Siggy may need to play defense."

He swallowed, nervously scratching his arm. "I-I won't let you down, sir."

"I know you won't. That's why I asked you to do it instead of Abby." I turned to the others. "Everyone ready?"

Josef, Abigail, and a team of trained soldiers stood before me, each one of them armed and ready for action. Even Dressler looked like she was ready to go to war, carrying that serious expression.

Josef stepped up. "The central core is located beneath us."

"We'll follow your lead," I said.

He smiled, heading for the nearest exit. The rest of us followed, except for Dressler, who doubled back toward Freddie.

I waited at the door for her while the others continued. "Something wrong?" I asked.

She paused, looking at me. I could tell she was debating something. "I…" She hesitated. "Back when you asked me to fix the engine, I…found something."

"Found what?" I asked, taking a step closer.

"I couldn't fix the engine. I'm not a specialist in slip drives," she explained. "However, I do have some experience with cloaks. I spent a few years designing them."

I raised an eye. "You looked at my cloak?"

"Not for long, but I noticed it was Union design. It's easy to spot if you know the type," she said, but then waved her hands. "Anyway, after you and Abigail left the ship, Frederick and I had nothing but time, so I focused on a way to disable the transponder. It wasn't difficult."

"You fixed my cloak?" I asked. I couldn't believe what I was hearing. "Why didn't you tell me about this?"

She scoffed. "Why do you think? I wasn't even sure if I should disable it in the first place, except that if the Union found you, they'd attack, and frankly, I didn't want to die by association."

"You only disabled the cloak in order to save yourself?" asked Freddie.

"I know it sounds horrible, but you're a bunch of criminals. What would you do?"

"Probably the same thing," I admitted.

"I was still debating if I should reactivate it, to be honest," she admitted. "But after you turned over that

Tritium core...after seeing all of you risk your lives for these people..." She paused and took a breath. "Well, you get the point."

"I don't think I do," I said, walking closer to her. "I think I need you to clarify it for me, Doc."

She rolled her eyes. "You know exactly what I was saying. Don't play stupid." She walked past me. "Let's go before we're left behind."

Freddie and I watched her head into the tunnel. "I think she's warming up to us," Fred said.

"They always do," I answered with a sly grin.

THE RESIDENTS WATCHED us running through the halls, probably wondering what was going on. They'd find out soon, whenever Janus and Karin explained the situation. I couldn't help but wonder if they'd even understand. A massive carrier ship from an unknown empire was on its way to destroy them? Why would anyone want to do such a thing?

I envied their ignorance, in a way. Despite the dangerous world they'd found themselves on, it was far enough away from the rest of the galaxy to keep them in a bubble, all to themselves. They had never heard about Sarkonians, the Union, or Renegades before.

Maybe that was my fault. I was the one who dropped my ship on their world, after all. If I hadn't come along, they might have lived the rest of their lives without ever discovering the outside universe.

Oh well. What was done was done, and there was no going back. Not for me and certainly not for them. They'd have to make their stand right here, with my crew beside them, for better or worse.

Josef led us down a flight of stairs, deeper into another corridor. Janus had activated emergency lighting to guide us, which was better than nothing.

As we neared another stairwell, I heard my comm activate. "Captain, do you read me?" asked Freddie.

"I've got you. What's going on?"

"Sigmond says the Union is on their way here," he said.

"Correct," said Sigmond. "The *Galactic Dawn* has set course for this planet and should arrive momentarily."

I kept running, along with the rest of the team, shuffling down the stairs. "I want you to get to a safe location. Stay cloaked and don't fire unless you get my order. Do you understand, Fred?"

"I-I understand!" he answered.

"Now stay off the damn comm!" I snapped. "I gotta focus on—"

The wall exploded straight ahead, sending pieces of metal and rock onto the floor. Dust scattered, and we shuffled back and away.

Josef was ahead of me, leading the way. He nearly stumbled forward as the break occurred, but I managed to grab hold of his shoulder and pull.

A figure leapt into the storm, swiping claws and roaring. The monster grabbed the nearest soldier, digging a claw right into the poor bastard's belly, skewering him like a piece of meat.

The rest of us opened fire, lighting up the corridor with so much firepower, it was a wonder the whole structure didn't come down on us.

The soldiers let loose several blasts of energy from their spears, spilling the Boneclaw's guts in seconds. By far the most efficient kill I'd seen so far.

It collapsed in its own blood, half its abdomen missing, with the soldier still on its claw. The man was dead—you could see by the empty look in his eyes—but we couldn't leave him there. Two of the others pulled him off and set him against the other wall, checking his pulse to be certain.

I expected some kind of ritual, but there was nothing. Only a brief moment of silence as his friends—people he must have known his entire life—closed his eyes and placed his hands in his lap.

No goodbye. No tears. All of it was treated so casually.

Watching them, I couldn't help but wonder if all of this was normal—if they'd lived their lives so long with pain that perhaps it was all they knew.

In that moment, I thought of Lex...

And I thanked the gods I didn't believe in that she never had to live in a place as terrible as this.

19

WE FOUND the system core room in less than fifteen
minutes, having raced through three stairwells and seven
floors.

Josef entered a code into the door pad, finally giving us
access. Inside, the dim orange lights along the upper walls
gave the area a soft ambiance that was almost relaxing. If I
hadn't known any better, I might have said it was almost
peaceful.

But that was before I saw the little piles of bones, scattered along the floor.

"Jace..." muttered Abigail.

I held up my hand, whispering, "Josef, were these here
the last time you visited?"

"No," the old man responded. "This is new."

I glanced at the nearest soldier. "Same for you?"

The soldier nodded.

"Everyone, stay alert," I said, keeping my voice low. "Let's go."

We crept through the room, minding the bones at our feet, trying not to step on them. Straight ahead of us, a short set of stairs ascended to a platform. I could already see the machine at the back of it, the focal point of this place, the entire reason for its existence.

But around us, along the walls, I saw several tunnel openings where the animals had burrowed inside. We'd found a kind of nest, and the only question was whether it was active or not.

We reached the stairs in seconds, which ascended to the second platform. I could almost feel my heart beating in my chest as I took them, one after the next.

Finally, the machine came into view. We were there at last, less than twenty meters away.

But between us, I saw another collection of bones, only this time, they were different.

"Oh, my gods," whispered Dressler. She was staring at the same thing I was, at the human skulls resting at the center of several piles. Unlike the previous collections, these were decidedly human.

"Easy," I said, looking at the doctor.

But her eyes were frantic, and I could see the fear as it built inside of her. "Th-this is barbaric," she said, her voice shaking. "They're monsters! They—"

I grabbed her by the shoulder. "Will hear you if you don't shut up!"

"B-but—"

Abigail was right beside me. She took the doctor by her wrist gently and gave her a calming look, like a mother trying to calm a child.

Dressler swallowed, giving a slight nod.

I motioned for the machine, letting everyone know to keep going.

That was when I heard it.

THUMK.

The cracking sound echoed through the room. We each turned behind us, looking at one of the soldiers near the rear of the group. He gave us a confused expression, looking down at his feet. There were no broken bones there, nothing to indicate he'd taken the wrong step.

THUMK.

We all stared at each other, not moving. The echo had come from another location, but I couldn't place it.

THUMK.

THUMK.

I raised my eyes to the rear of the room, toward the machine. The sound seemed to be coming from there.

A shadow moved, slightly behind the side of it, small and slow, edging its way out.

I extended my hand across Dressler's chest, pushing her behind me, and readied my weapon. Abigail did the same, along with the rest of the soldiers as we watched and waited.

A figure appeared, half a meter tall, covered in white fur. It looked like a baby Boneclaw, flicking its ears as it bent its head at us. We watched it curiously as the animal waddled forward and into the middle of the room.

Its claws were underdeveloped, I quickly noticed, but it was certainly the same creature as the others. The dark area where its eyes should be gave that away.

"Chuchukuu," it said in a squeaky voice.

Abigail breathed a sigh of relief, lowering her weapon. "Mighty gods, kill me now."

"It's just a runt," I said, taking a step closer.

As I did, I felt a hand on my arm. "Wait," said Josef.

I looked back at him. "What is it? Is that thing gonna spit poison at me? I wouldn't be surprised."

"No, but Boneclaws never abandon their young for very long. The mother will be back soon," he explained.

"Just one?" I asked.

He nodded. "I suspect this is a nest. Only the mother will be here with the cubs."

"That's a relief," I said.

He shook his head. "You haven't seen the mothers, have you?"

"Let's not wait around for her, then," said Abigail. She retrieved the Tritium core from her pack and handed it to Josef. "Hurry."

He took the core in his hands. "Of course. Janus, are you there? Can you hear me?"

"I am receiving you," said the Cognitive, his voice coming from a nearby speaker.

"Please open the barrier so that I can replace the core," said Jo.

"Stand by," said Janus.

The machine in front of us began to emit a low humming sound. It startled the little Boneclaw, causing him to scurry back. "Chu!" it exclaimed, nearly falling on its rear. "Chuchukuu!"

The protective first metal layer moved in front of the machine, shifting into the nearby wall.

The second layer followed, and then the third, each one sliding and disappearing as the central access point revealed itself. Whoever had built this machine knew how deadly a Tritium core could be, so having it secured had been a top priority. Letting the wrong person get their hands on an energy source like this would spell disaster.

It was a good thing, then, that the Union had never found a way to replicate Lex's tattoos. If they had, the galaxy would never have been the same.

Instead, I'd given that power to a senile old man I'd found in a cave.

It was the right decision.

Josef stepped up to the machine and tapped the controls, entering a code. The light inside came alive, and a small, translucent piece of glass slid back, presenting another core to him.

He looked at me for confirmation. "Do it," I said firmly.

Josef nodded, taking the old core out of the slot.

The machine responded by going silent, all the lights completely fading. He handed the device to Abigail, who placed it inside her pack. Next, he slid the new core inside, setting it horizontally and letting it snap into place.

The machine roared when he did, filling the room with a monstrous hum. It was so loud, I couldn't hear Abigail when she tried to speak.

"What?" I asked.

She pointed to her ear, trying again to say something.

Josef stepped back from the machine, letting the sliding doors fall back into place and shielding his ears.

I grabbed the old man by the shoulders and shouted in his face. "What the hell is happening?!"

"It's restarting!" he yelled back. "Just wait!"

Right at that moment, the noise stopped, and the room was suddenly quiet. The lights along the upper walls grew brighter too, replacing the dim, drained color from before.

"Chu!" shouted the little Boneclaw.

Dressler looked at me, still holding her ears. "That was the worst startup sequence I've ever seen!"

"Apologies," said Janus, materializing before us. "The system needed to cycle itself before it could activate the new core."

The soldiers reacted to his sudden appearance by raising their weapons. It only took a second for them to realize who he was.

"I guess that means the emitters are working for you," I said.

The Cognitive smiled. "It would seem so. Thank you all very much."

"What's next?" asked Abby.

"Karin has authorized the use of long-range missiles," said Janus. "Please return to the upper floor while I begin the activation process. It will take several minutes."

"Janus, how strong are your defenses?" I asked. "Can you really stop something as powerful as the *Galactic Dawn*?"

"If the missiles are still in working order, I expect we'll make a good show of it, to say the least," he said.

"Chu!" yelled the little Boneclaw. "Chu chu!"

I felt a sudden vibration in the grate beneath my feet.

THOMB.

"Chu!" shouted the tiny animal.

Another vibration.

THOMB.

I slowly looked at Abigail. "Mommy's back."

"Everyone, get ready to defend yourselves!" said Janus.

The soldiers formed a small circle around us, but I pushed the nearest one aside. "Out of my way," I muttered, refusing to let someone else do the dirty work for me.

The baby Boneclaw cried again. "Chuchukoo!"

THOMB.

THOMB.

THOMB.

I could feel every step the creature made, so much stronger than the others. So much bigger.

The tunnel trembled as it came, dust falling from the stones.

The monster's hands were smaller than the others, its claws about half the size. It walked on four legs, carrying the bulk of its weight at the fat center.

The mother's ears flickered as it approached, stopping at the mouth of the tunnel, letting out a quick yelp. "Eepo! Eepo!"

The little infant waddled over to its feet. "Chu! Chu!"

The mother's backside split apart. Six legs extended from inside, like the legs of an insect, and she picked up the child with them, placing it on her back.

I wasn't sure what to do. We couldn't run without her noticing, possibly starting a fight, but an outright attack might create other problems.

We kept our weapons aimed on the monster, waiting to see what it did. I could sense the soldier next to me breathing heavily, shifting where he stood.

The Boneclaw tilted its head, flicking its ears several times. It took a step towards us but paused, waiting.

I swallowed the lump in my throat as a bead of sweat ran down my neck. I could hear the other soldiers beside me, nervously fidgeting. *She knows we're here*, I thought, observing the creature.

The mother stepped back, retracted her insect legs to cover the infant in her pouch. She let out a quick "Eepo," to which the child replied, "Chu." Then the animal turned away and headed into the tunnel, leaving us behind. The floor shook as she stomped away, further into the darkness.

"O-oh gods," muttered Dressler.

"Why didn't it attack?" asked Abby.

"Maybe she was protecting the child," said Dressler. "An attack would only endanger it."

I let myself breathe, trying to loosen my nerves. "Let's just get the hell out of this place. I've had my fill of this nightmare."

20

WE MADE it back in one piece, no Boneclaws to slow us down this time. Good thing, since the *Galactic Dawn* was about to be in orbit.

"We're tracking the ship now," said Freddie, his voice coming through the comm. The *Renegade Star* was floating in close orbit, cloaked, and staying out of sight. "It's still on course for the planet."

"Specifically, your current position, sir," inserted Siggy.

I cursed, shaking my head. "Don't get too close if you can help it. Stand by for now."

"Understood," Siggy answered.

I looked at Karin as we all stood around the conference room table. "We need options."

Janus materialized beside her. "Weapons systems are coming online. So far, they appear to be operational."

"Get ready to use them," I told him.

"There's something else," said the Cognitive. "I believe I can activate the station's shield, or part of it, at least."

"What's that mean? What part?" asked Abigail.

"The shield was created to conceal all three facilities, but it relied on all three Tritium cores to function. Since the other two stations no longer have working cores, I can only use—"

"The new core," finished Dressler. Her eyes widened. "If you do that, you could drain the core's energy."

"It is a possibility," said Janus.

"I thought it was fully charged," I said.

"It is," said Janus. "However, the core would be outputting at three times its intended capacity. Tritium cores are meant to recharge automatically while in use. If they exceed their intended output, the result could be full depletion."

"Could you limit the size of the shield?" asked Dressler. She'd been standing behind me until now, saying nothing. "Bring it down to only this section."

"Yes, I believe that might be possible, although that is not the only problem," said Janus.

"What else?" I asked.

Janus flicked his wrist, changing the image of the wall to show the *Galactic Dawn*, finally orbiting the planet. "If this ship is as powerful as you claim, it stands to reason it may bombard the shield. Given the decay of the architecture here, it's unlikely to last for very long."

"But it can work," I said.

The Cognitive nodded. "For a time."

"When you say your systems are back online, does that include communications?" asked Dressler.

"How do you mean?" he asked.

"Long range," she said. "Off planet. Out of system."

"Had you asked me that a thousand years ago, I might have said yes," continued Janus. "Now, however, I simply do not know."

Dressler was quiet for a moment, scratching her ear. "Hm."

I found myself waiting for her to continue, the tension in the air only getting thicker by the second. "For gods' sake, Doc, what the hell are you on about?" I finally blurted out.

She flinched at the question. "Ah, sorry, Captain. I was thinking." Dressler's eyes fell on Janus. "Could you send a signal out, long range, in all directions? Something that only an old Earth vessel might pick up?"

"That would depend on how well the communication systems are after all this time," said the Cognitive.

"But if they work, you can do it?" she asked.

He nodded. "Certainly."

Dressler shot a wicked look at me. "*That's* the answer. We send a message to *Titan* and give them our location. It's the best chance we have."

The suggestion took me by surprise. I had never thought of trying that. If it worked, Athena and the others might actually be able to swoop in and save us. "Do you think you can do that, Janus?" I finally asked.

"I believe I can try," he answered.

"Hold on," inserted Karin. "Everything you're saying… it sounds like we're going to war with these people. Do you really think it will come to that? Isn't it at least *possible* we could speak to them and work something out?"

Abigail answered this time. "This world is worth more than anything they've ever come across. They'll do whatever it takes to harvest it."

Karin's eyes dropped to the table. "After all this time, our first contact with the rest of the galaxy is going to be hostile." She sighed. "How fitting for us."

"You can survive this," I said.

"How?" she asked. "From everything you've told me about these people, they have more resources. We're using the remnants of what our ancestors left behind. None of that equipment has been maintained. We don't even have any ships."

"Ships," I muttered, almost to myself.

"What was that, Jace?" asked Abby.

I hadn't thought about it before, but the shuttle was still on the *Renegade Star*. It couldn't be used because we were so far away from *Titan*, but maybe now, with the new core in place…

"Janus, do you know anything about the ship I had on the *Star*?" I asked.

"The short-range attack vessel?" he asked.

"That's the one. Looks like a giant triangle," I said.

"I'm well versed in pre-colonization era technology."

"Now that we've got that core online, is it possible to start the ship up again?" I asked.

"Ah, yes," he said. "The connector links were taken offline, but they should be available now."

I tapped my ear. "Siggy, Freddie, get your asses back down here! I need that strike ship you've got in your belly!"

"You want us back on the surface?" asked Freddie.

"Captain, what are you doing?" asked Karin.

"Yes, please share," said Dressler.

"No celebrating yet, ladies," I said, already feeling my heart begin to race. "But godsdamn, I just might have an idea."

AFTER A LENGTHY DISCUSSION, it seemed we had a plan.

Or at least, something close to one. Everything depended on the old communication systems still being operational. The rest existed solely to buy us more time.

Abigail and I ran through the facility, back to the field, leaving Dressler behind to help Karin and the others with getting the communication network back online.

I met Freddie outside in the snow. He was waiting with a nervous look in his eyes, no doubt frantic over the looming threat hanging above us in orbit. "What's your plan, Captain?" he asked as I raced into the cargo bay. I went to the ancient strike ship and touched the door.

A wave of relief washed over me as my tattoos began to glow. It was as I had hoped. The ship was operational again, thanks to the new Tritium core in the facility.

The door cracked open, sliding up to give me access. "Keep the *Star* cloaked and follow me," I ordered. "Don't engage the enemy unless you think you have to. You got that, Fred?"

"I think so," said Freddie.

"Abby here will take the guns, same as last time," I said, nodding to her.

"Leave it to us," she said.

"Uh, why are we doing this?" asked Freddie. "It's suicide to take on the Union, isn't it?"

"We're going to buy some time and hope that Janus and the others can get a signal out to *Titan*," I explained.

"*Titan?*" he asked. "Are you serious?"

I gave him a wicked grin, climbing into the ship. "Don't I *look* serious?"

The interior of the strike ship was already alive with activity, waiting for me to activate the controls. I took a seat and placed my hand on the dash, trying to clear my mind. It had been a few days since I used this thing, and even then, I barely had any training.

The craft began to rise from the cargo bay floor, hovering gently in the air. Freddie watched from the locker area. I tapped my ear with my free hand, saying, "Get us in the air, Fred. Keep us cloaked."

He nodded then ran to the rear of the room and up the stairs. I let the vessel settle back to the floor, returning to its standby position.

Abby lingered there a moment, watching me from the corner of the room. I could see the concern in her eyes as it slowly began to form and build. The risk was right before us, and this time, we didn't have *Titan* there to help us. We didn't even have a working slipspace engine. Worse still, there were hundreds of people on this planet whose lives depended on our success.

I forced a smile as I gave her a confident look. She did the same.

As the engines ignited beneath our feet and the *Renegade Star* lifted from the snow-covered earth, I couldn't help but think about how so much had changed in such a short amount of time.

For all of us.

And I'd be damned if I was going to let it all die.

21

THE RENEGADE STAR flew through the sky with just enough speed to avoid detection by the *Galactic Dawn*'s sensors. If we drew too close, they'd be able to read our engine's heat signature, but at this distance, we'd be safe enough to break orbit.

That also meant we had to fly a hundred or so kilometers in another direction—east, in this case—just so we didn't wind up running straight into them.

We entered orbit and cut the engines, setting the ship on a path to meet the *Dawn* in less than fifteen minutes.

"Pop the doors, Siggy," I ordered, placing my hand on the dash of the strike ship once again. It hovered off the floor.

"Right away, sir," said the A.I.

The cargo bay door cracked and slowly descended. I

moved the ship forward, through the room and out into open space. Once free, I turned myself around to see the inside of the *Star*, like a floating portal in the middle of space. The door began to close, causing the light from the cargo bay to slowly bend and fade, allowing the cloak to fully shield the ship once again.

I brought the vessel away and headed closer to the *Dawn*. I knew they wouldn't detect me, given the nature of these ancient Earth ships, but I decided to stay cautious anyway, just in case, and keep enough distance to run if I had to.

"Sir, please be advised, the *Galactic Dawn* is sending a transmission to the surface of the planet," informed Sigmond.

"What kind of transmission?" I asked.

"It appears to be a video stream. Shall I play it?" he asked. "I can relay the stream to your dashboard holo."

"Go ahead," I said.

The feed appeared in front of me, and with it, a familiar face. "Attention, Captain Hughes and anyone else who might be hearing this. Respond immediately. We have your location and the coordinates of the facility or base you are using. Answer now or we *will* open fire."

General Brigham spoke with authority, but he couldn't hide his anger. It was there, deep in his eyes, waiting to be unleashed. If I gave him the chance, he'd slit my throat with his own hands.

"Siggy," I said, shutting off the holo with only a

thought. "Keep monitoring that ship and let me know if anything else happens with it."

"Of course, sir," said the A.I.

I told the ship to open a line to Janus. A few seconds later, another holo appeared—this time, of Janus's face. "Hello, Captain."

"What's your status?" I asked.

"With Doctor Dressler's assistance, I believe we can re-establish our communication system. She and a small team are currently on their way to make the necessary repairs."

"You think she can handle it?" I asked.

"She is most proficient," he answered. "I am confident we will have the system online soon."

"What about the shield?" I asked.

"Modifications have been made and we are ready to deploy," he said.

"Do it," I ordered.

He nodded. "Activating now. The enemy ship has also been targeted. When you're ready to attack, please give the word and we will do the same."

I thought about the base, not realizing that it would change the holo. An imenage appeared of the surface, showing me the entire base as it was, and I saw a sudden wave of blue energy form from the ground up, like a bubble. It looked identical to *Titan*'s shield, translucent with a blue tint.

"Activation sequence successful," Janus said.

"Stand by," I told him. "Get ready to launch those missiles."

"Understood," he said, and then the comm switched off.

I sat there, floating in the dead of space, waiting for the moment. I wouldn't initiate this fight, because that would only bring the resolution faster, and Janus needed all the time he could get to send that message out. The longer it took for these bastards to wise up and attack the base, the better off we'd all—

Brigham appeared on my dash again. "We see you have activated a shield," he said. "If you do not deactivate it and hand yourselves over, we will proceed with the attack. You have ten seconds to respond."

I leaned forward, and my ship moved with me, its engines igniting with more power than intended. I exploded toward the enemy carrier and aimed my guns directly at their forward quad cannons.

"Suit yourselves," said General Brigham, shaking his head. "Begin bombardment."

The holo faded right as I neared the ship. I could already see the cannons turning, getting ready to fire. A light formed, releasing a blast of firepower so large, I wagered it could have destroyed an entire city block.

The projectiles hit the shield, sending ripples down the side of the circle as four explosions formed.

I brought my ship within firing distance of the cannons and ordered the vessel to attack. At once, a single blue beam erupted, hitting the *Galactic Dawn* and breaking two of the guns in half.

"Janus, now!" I snapped, moving my ship to the next set of cannons. "Fire!"

"Understood," said the Cognitive.

The holo showed dozens of missiles, leaving a section of the facility I'd never seen before. Most of it had been buried in the snow until now, when hidden silos emerged. Most fired successfully, sending a small fleet of unmanned bombs toward the invading vessel.

The *Galactic Dawn* raised its shield in response, trapping me inside, right after firing several of its own missiles to meet the others in the air. I couldn't help but feel like I'd been here before.

While Janus's weapons left the surface, I set my sights on taking out whatever vital systems I could find. I was completely out of mines, unlike the last time, but no matter. I'd find something to shoot, even if it killed me.

I took aim at the second set of quad cannons, commanding my ship to fire.

As my beam collided with the guns, the remaining missiles from the planet crashed into the *Dawn*'s shield, sending waves of ripples along the surface. Once it was over, the shield flickered out—deactivated but not destroyed, which meant something else was about to happen.

Sure enough, the *Galactic Dawn* lowered several of its doors, releasing swarms of strike ships, like insects from a hive. They bled into open space, flowing along the sides of the ship, moving toward me.

My position had been compromised.

"Janus, send the rest!" I barked, moving my ship away from the *Galactic Dawn*. "Freddie, Abigail, get ready!"

"Understood," said the Cognitive.

"Standing by!" said Abby.

The swarm followed me as I broke away from the ship, leading them toward the northern section of the planet, near the moon. Before I was too far, I turned around, cutting the engines to drift, and shot a single beam through the center of the mob.

Several of the ships exploded as the beam tore through them, while many more were set adrift.

The bulk of the ships came back together and continued after me, firing everything they had. "Stay cloaked, Freddie!" I ordered. "Don't show your cards just yet!"

"How long?" he asked.

"Just wait!" I told him.

I caught the moon's orbit, the swarm at my heels. The continued firing, but my ship was faster and more agile. They couldn't get a lock.

The holo revealed another silo as it opened, launching a series of missiles into the sky.

Now was my chance.

I led the enemy toward that location, moving into the atmosphere, but not too far.

The others followed, firing at my back. The hull shook with every hit, and I wondered briefly whether they might actually succeed in killing me.

But then I saw the missiles.

I crossed through the path of the missiles just in time for them to hit behind me, colliding with several hundred of the enemy strike ships.

The holo showed a widespread chain of explosions as the entire sky lit up and debris began to fall from the newly created wreckage. The blast lasted for several seconds. Those who weren't destroyed were either knocked off their flightpath or disabled and sent careening to the ground.

Several missiles managed to slip through, still, making their way to the *Dawn* in a second showing.

The bombs slammed into the shield, fracturing it. I raced through the clouds, re-entering space.

"Hot damn!" I barked, staring at the lights on my holo, each one representing a strike ship. Where there had been hundreds, now only a few dozen remained. The missile attack had decimated their numbers more than I ever could have dreamed. "Freddie, Abigail, time to take care of business!"

"On it, Captain!" responded Fred.

The *Renegade Star* decloaked in orbit, firing its quad cannons directly into a group of enemy vessels. A brief flash lit up the darkness, eviscerating three ships by the time the light settled.

The guns swiveled, unloading a spread of bullets on one vessel while the quad cannons targeted another.

With the *Star* picking up the stragglers, I set my sights on the *Dawn*.

As I brought my strike ship skyward, Brigham unleashed another bombardment on the base. "Janus, what's your status?" I signaled.

"Shields are holding," he responded. "Dr. Dressler successfully replaced a piece of faulty wiring, finally allowing me to activate the communications network."

"When are you sending the transmission?" I asked.

"I already did," he answered. "Thirty seconds ago. If Athena has an active receiver, she should detect the transmission shortly, even in slipspace."

The *Galactic Dawn* was right before me, actively priming its cannons, preparing for another bombardment. "Guess that means we still need to stall for time," I said, narrowing my eyes on the carrier ship. "Janus, you wouldn't be holding any more missiles in your back pocket, would you?"

"I'm afraid the arsenal has been depleted, Captain," said Janus. "You're on your own."

"Not a bad run," I said, taking out another set of quad cannons. There were only a few more left. With so many strike ships destroyed, along with the cannons, the *Dawn* would have no other choice but to stand down. We just had to keep whittling away at—

An alert blinked on my dash, informing me that a slip

tunnel had just opened. It was the one the *Dawn* had followed us with, which could only mean one thing.

Several indicator lights popped up, each one representing both Union and Sarkonian vessels.

"Shit," I muttered, watching the tear open and disappear as each new ship emerged.

In only a few minutes, three Union cruisers and eight Sarkonian fighters had arrived.

Things were about to get complicated.

"Freddie, form up on the *Dawn!*" I shouted. "Unload what you have before the others get here. Do as much damage as you can."

"On it," answered Freddie.

Our two ships converged on Brigham's, swiftly going after the last remaining quad cannons we could find. We might not be able to stop the others, but we could at least prevent the facility from getting bombed right away.

"Fleet arriving in two minutes," informed Sigmond. "I advise a swift retreat, sir."

"Not yet," I muttered, taking the strike ship to the front of the *Dawn*. Brigham had made several repairs since the last encounter, but I wagered there was little chance he'd completely fixed the hull, especially the section I'd blown to bits. Sure enough, sensors showed the hull was thinner here, still showing signs of decay. The repair crews had managed to replace the outer section of the hull, but there wasn't enough time to do the rest. If I could attack this point, maybe I could finally kill this bastard.

I ordered my ship to fire on that point, unleashing a blast of blue energy, only this time, it was precise, like a surgeon's scalpel. The hull began to split slowly, giving way to the beam. It would take some time for me to breach it like this, but it was the best chance I had.

"Sir, sensors are detecting a new slip tunnel forming near the sixth planet," said Sigmond.

"Say again, Siggy," I said.

"Another tear, sir. I show another ship emerging."

"Is it Union or Sarkonian?" I asked, bringing up the holo.

"Neither, sir. It appears to be…"

The holo lit up, showing a massive sphere emerging from the rift, pushing its way out. My eyes widened as I began to realize what I was looking at.

It was *Titan*, here at last.

22

I SMACKED THE DASH, briefly releasing control of the ship, overcome with relief. "There she is!" I snapped.

"Captain Hughes, this is Cognitive Athena of the colony seed ship *Titan*. Are you receiving?"

"I hear you," I answered, still firing the beam into the carrier ship in front of me.

"Scans show enemy vessels approaching your position," said Athena. "Shall I intervene?"

"Yes!" yelled Abigail. "For gods' sakes, yes!"

"Very well," said the Cognitive. "Setting course and deploying additional vessels to assist."

"Additional vessels?" asked Freddie.

The holo zoomed in on the moon, indicating three new lights as they emerged from *Titan*.

"Everyone doing okay?" asked a voice on the other end.

"Is that Alphonse?" asked Freddie.

"It is," he answered. "But I'm not alone."

"Octavia here," said another voice.

"And Bolin," said the third.

"Well, this is a surprise," said Abigail. "It appears we've all been a little busy since our last meet up."

"Let's exchange stories later," I said. "Focus on the other ships. Alphonse, Octavia, and Bolin, protect the planet. That's the priority."

"Understood," said Alphonse. "We're on our way."

"Why the planet?" asked Octavia.

"There are people down there," said Abigail. "People like Lex."

"Oh? Well, that's interesting," said Alphonse. "Captain, what's the preferred attack pattern?"

"Take out the Sarkonians first," I ordered. "They're smaller, faster. We can let Athena worry about the cruisers."

"Understood," said Alphonse.

The three strike ships set their sights on the fleet and took off, firing three beams at once, cutting a swath through several of the ships.

I focused my attention on the *Galactic Dawn*. I wasn't going to let Brigham lay another trap for me. Not today.

The *Renegade Star* joined the others, cloaking as it moved, and then uncloaking long enough to fire a cannon before disappearing again. Nothing like a little hide-and-seek to keep them guessing.

"Captain, I am transferring your vessel's connection to

Titan," said Athena. "It appears the current source is becoming unstable."

"Unstable?" I asked. "Come again?"

"Scans are showing instability in the facility's Tritium core unit, like due to the strain of the shield. Were you not aware?" she asked.

I called up Janus immediately. His face appeared on the holo, the same as before. "Is everything okay down there?" I quickly asked.

"Apologies, Captain," he said. "We are experiencing some strain on the system. Karin is initiating emergency evacuation procedures."

"Where is she taking everyone?" I asked.

"To the third facility, using a path on the surface. The core is becoming unstable. Should we continue to take damage, a full collapse may occur."

"What does that mean, a full collapse?" I asked.

He gave me knowing look. "The end of this facility, I'm afraid."

"Shit," I whispered. "What kind of blast radius would that be?"

"Unknown," said the Cognitive.

"Captain, if I may," inserted Athena, her disembodied voice coming from all around me. "Greetings, Janus. Please forgive the lack of pleasantries, but if I might make a suggestion."

"Welcome to the neighborhood," said Janus.

"Thank you," said Athena. "If I can move *Titan* close

enough, I may be able to send transport vessels to the ground."

"I thought you couldn't fly the ships without a pilot," I said.

"Correct," she said. "However, the ships can be directed automatically, using *Titan's* energy beams. I'm afraid this will lower the strength of our shield temporarily, but my calculations show it to be the optimal solution."

"That works for me," I said. "Janus?"

"Indeed," he answered. "Athena, I'm transferring coordinates to you now for extraction. Thank you."

"You are welcome," she said.

According to the radar, the cruisers were nearly upon us, set to arrive shortly after *Titan*. If we didn't hurry and handle the situation soon, a whole lot of people were going to wind up dead.

I BROKE through the outer hull of the *Galactic Dawn*, right as *Titan* arrived. My sensors informed me when I'd breached the first deck, which, from what I could tell, seemed to be the cargo hold.

Titan arrived and released a small fleet of ships to the surface of the planet. In response, the *Galactic Dawn* fired several point-defense turrets at the moon's shield. Without access to their quad cannons, however, there was little they could do.

At the same time, *Titan*'s energy seemed to be too focused on rescue and defense to retaliate properly, which meant it could only sit there and take the constant attack.

One of the Sarkonian ships broke through the others, hastily approaching my position. It fired a string of blasts, giving me only a few seconds to get out of there.

I commanded my ship to cut the beam and evade, but not before one of the projectiles struck my side, knocking me into a spin. As I righted myself, I caught sight of the other projectiles and quickly ordered my ship to dive.

I flew toward the surface, turning as I reached the stratosphere, then used the atmospheric friction to carry me as I ignited my thrusters and pushed away.

As the torpedoes neared, I ordered my ship to release its flak into space, catching the projectiles and immediately igniting them behind me.

Only the Sarkonian vessel remained. I raised myself away and cut my engines, turning my ship around to face it. With a simple command, I shot my beam cannon and sent a steady blast toward the ship right as it came into view.

The bastard didn't stand a chance.

Before I could celebrate, Janus's face materialized on my holo. "Captain, all members of the colony have boarded and await departure."

"Athena?" I called. "You hearing this?"

"Understood," she answered, immediately. "Thank you, Janus. Stand by for extraction."

"Janus, are you there with Karin?" I asked.

"Karin is on board one of the vessels, along with Lucia, Josef, and everyone else," he said.

"But what about you?" I asked.

"I'm afraid I do not possess the ability to leave this station," he explained.

I paused, surprised by the statement. "Are you…are you sure?"

"Quite," he replied. "I apologize for the inconvenience, Captain, but it is simply unavoidable. My processes are tied directly to the system. I cannot be moved, barring—"

"Athena!" I snapped. "Do something!"

"I may be able to initiate a transfer override, given enough time," she said.

"Janus, you hear that?" I asked. "Hold on a bit longer!"

"I'm afraid that won't work either," he said. "The core will fail at any moment. Shutting it down would only create a meltdown, potentially destroying the ships before they have a chance to leave. I must maintain my position."

"Shut the fucking thing off!" I barked. "Janus, we can still save—"

The holo flickered, distorting Janus's face for a brief moment before finally adjusting. He seemed to look right at me, straight into my eyes. "Look after them, Jace Hughes," he said, and a gentle smile warmed his face. "I leave the rest to you."

"Janus!" I shouted, reaching for the holo right as it broke apart.

Suddenly, the surface of the planet filled with a flash of light, leaving the largest mushroom cloud I'd ever seen to spread across the sky.

THE CRUISERS FIRED everything they had at *Titan*. Athena extended the range of her shield to safeguard the other ships as they arrived. This was going to take a few minutes, and I was certain that shield wouldn't be able to last.

"Everyone, form up on me," I ordered.

"What's the plan, Captain?" asked Alphonse.

"Target the first cruiser. Between the four of us, we should be able to do some damage and buy Athena some time."

"What about us?" asked Abigail.

"Use the cloak like you've been doing. Cover our backs and let us take most of the heat," I said. "Look for any stray ships. I don't need another surprise Sarkonian firing rockets up my ass again."

"You can count on the two of us!" exclaimed Freddie.

"Three," corrected Sigmond.

"Right!" said Fred.

The *Renegade Star* cloaked while the rest of us opened fire on the nearest cruiser. Four sharp beams cut through the front cannons and swept across the hull, making fast work of its armaments. The cruiser tried to retaliate, but they were having a tough time of it, firing blindly in every direction.

A second later, the docking bay opened and out poured a small squadron of fighters. Before they could make it very far, however, Alphonse and Octavia were there, blasting through them and into the bay itself.

Bolin followed from behind, ramming himself straight into the interior. His beam ignited everything in sight, creating a tide of blue fire along the deck and into the nearby corridors. Emergency systems activated the extinguishers, but it was too late. Half the bay had already been destroyed.

My sensors detected hundreds of dots—escape pods—leaving the cruiser. That was odd, since I was sure we hadn't done enough damage to justify them abandoning ship.

The pods ignited their thrusters and flew toward the rear-most cruiser. "They're running!" exclaimed Bolin.

"Keep your focus on this one," I said. "We'll move to the second as soon as we—"

A white light engulfed my vision as the cruiser exploded, breaking into pieces. The force threw me back into my seat, bringing my hand off the control.

I spun out of control, away from the debris and toward the planet.

23

I BLACKED out for only a few seconds, but it was long enough to forget where I was and what I'd been doing.

I could barely move as the ship spiraled out of control. How had I gotten here? What was this sick feeling in my stomach? Was I about to die?

My eyes darted around the ship, searching for a solution. I tried to speak, but the strain was too much on me. I could barely even move.

I raised my arm from the seat slowly, pushing it with everything I had, trying to reach the dash. Trying...

I clenched my teeth, grasping at the air, bending my fingers. Almost there.

My hand graced the edge of the dash, a blue light forming beneath my fingertips. "Stop!" I finally managed to scream.

Thrusters activated, bringing me to a full stop in mid-air, the force of which hurt my ass, it was so strong.

Up, I thought. *Go up!*

The ship exploded forward, rising back into the sky, exchanging blue for black as I left the stratosphere.

The radar showed the cruiser had been completely destroyed, but I was still reading two others, along with the *Galactic Dawn*. More importantly, four more dots, each of them blue, showed that my crew was still alive, or at the very least, their ships were still transmitting. "Everyone! Report!"

"W-we're okay," said Freddie.

"I was far enough away to avoid it," said Alphonse.

"I'm okay," reported Octavia.

There was a short pause.

"Bolin?" I asked.

No response.

"Bolin! Answer me, godsdammit!" I snapped.

"C-captain Hughes," he said, his voice cracking.

I exhaled, relaxing in my chair.

"C-can't move the ship," he muttered. "Engines are down."

"Bolin, are you hurt?" asked Octavia.

"Yes," he said in a low voice.

"Stay where you are," she said. "Sigmond, can you pick him up?"

"Affirmative," answered the A.I.

One of the cruisers was moving again, heading in front

of the third, no doubt to block the escape pods as they loaded into the third ship's landing bay. "Looks like we've got more problems," I said. "Siggy, take care of Bolin. Everyone else, we're not done yet."

"Captain, this is Athena," I heard her voice declare. "All colonists are safely aboard *Titan*. Please retreat to the ship. Let me take it from here."

"Not until we have Bolin on the *Star!*" I said. "Everyone, cover them. The second they have that ship, get out of here!"

"Understood!" said Alphonse.

"Athena, start moving to meet that cruiser! Get your glorious fat ass between us," I said.

We moved quickly, flying to meet the cruiser before it reached Bolin's position. It launched multiple quad cannon missiles, each one heading for its own target.

Octavia fired a beam, destroying two of them in the process, while Alphonse and I took the rest. Our three beams intersected, leaping from one bomb to the next as the cruiser continued to deliver what seemed like an endless stream of firepower.

The *Star* arrived behind us, cloaking itself and lowering the cargo bay door. Sensors showed a tow cable extending out to Bolin, catching the nose and pulling him in. It was going to take some time to load his ship. Maybe too long.

I activated the comm. "Siggy, patch me through to the *Galactic Dawn.*"

"Yes, sir. Please hold," said the A.I. After a short pause, he said, "Go ahead."

"General Brigham, this is Captain Hughes of the *Renegade Star*. Tell your cruisers to stand down."

The holo changed to show Brigham's face and torso. "There you are," he said. "Captain Hughes, at last, you've finally decided to surrender yourself. Better late than never."

"Shut the hell up and listen to me, Brigham. Either you have your people stand down or that moon-sized ship is going to clear a hole straight through the middle of your stomach. Are you hearing me?" I asked.

"If that *thing* could have attacked, it would have done so by now," he said, shaking his head. "No, I believe you're at your end, Captain."

I sighed. "Athena, can you—"

Before I could finish the sentence, a beam struck the *Dawn*'s hull, forming another breach. Atmosphere began to vent immediately as the automated systems locked the section down. "Done," said Athena.

I quickly checked her position. She was growing closer to us, but not so far that she couldn't fire a second beam if I needed it.

"Hear that?" I asked, looking at the man on the holo. "Try me again."

The old man's eyes showed a glimpse of horror before straightening, returning to the same calm demeanor as before. "Tell Commander Braxin to stand down!"

"But, sir!" said someone I couldn't see.

"Do it!" the general ordered.

"That's more like it," I said, giving him a smile.

"Captain, you listen to me. If you don't turn yourself in, the Union will not stop its pursuit. We will hunt you forever, if that's what it takes. You're only putting more people in harm's way by——"

"By what?" I asked, leaning closer to the holo. "Keeping my crew away from you?"

"Defying the Union is not a viable, long-term solution, Captain. Even if you killed me here and now, the other fleets would come." He shook his head. "In fact, they're already on their way."

"Other fleets?" I asked.

"That's right, Hughes. Nothing you do here or in the future can stop what's coming. The Union will have its prize, even if it costs them an armada. When the dust has settled, and everyone is dead, that weapon you call a child will be back in their possession. They will hunt you to the ends of the galaxy. Perhaps even beyond."

I felt my chest tighten and my shoulders tense. The end of the galaxy? Would I have to go on the run like this for the rest of my life? I swallowed. No, I had to find a way out of this nonsense. A way to either kill the Union or exile it back into the hole it grew out of.

"Maybe you're right," I muttered. "Maybe you'll win in the end and I'll be dead tomorrow and that'll be it, but tomorrow isn't today." I gave him a crooked smile. "Today, you're the one who's lost."

In an instant, five blue lights erupted from *Titan*, forming a single, central beam at its center, firing into the second cruiser.

The ship's underbelly tore apart, its twelve hulls splitting open like a filleted fish.

As the beam dissipated, another formed, latching on to the *Star* and its new passenger, pulling it inside *Titan* at once.

The rest of us quickly followed, making our escape. My radar showed several cannons firing on us from the third cruiser, sending a spread of missiles towards us.

But I was already inside the perimeter of the shield as it went up, encasing *Titan* and all its people, right as the torpedoes hit.

Before I could even land the damn strike ship, I ordered Athena to open a tunnel and get us the hell out of there.

"Activating slip drive," the Cognitive answered. "Stand by."

The rift formed in seconds, breaking the darkness apart and replacing it with emerald light. I brought my ship into the landing bay, the new rift at my back. It was a sight to behold after days spent underground. I wanted to rest, to go and have a hot meal or a stiff drink. But more than anything, I realized, I wanted to see my crew.

Titan entered the tunnel quickly, maintaining our shields

as the third cruiser continued its attack, giving us everything it had.

But it was too late. After another series of missiles hit the shield, we were already halfway through the opening.

IN MINUTES, the rift had closed behind us, sealing the enemy for however long we might have. "Give me a head count, Athena," I said as my ship settled and locked itself in place. I lowered my head and closed my eyes, trying to steady my breathing.

"All passengers accounted for," she informed me.

"And Bolin?" I asked.

"He is being taken by Abigail Pryar and Frederick Tabernacle to a medical pod."

"Is he still alive?" I asked.

"Yes," she said, and I felt myself relax at the sound of the word. "Rest assured, he will recover, Captain."

I watched several of the colonists running through the landing bay. I couldn't believe we'd done it. They were all still alive, still talking.

Laughter rang from nearby. "Mister Hughes!"

I looked and saw Lex, running up with open arms. She hit me so hard, I nearly fell back, but it was good. I laughed. "Easy there," I told her, but she only smiled at me.

"You're back!" she exclaimed, hugging me with all the

strength a kid can muster. "Where did you go? What took you so long?"

I could sense the strain in her voice as she spoke. The concern and relief, all happening at once. It was too much for a child. I stepped back so I could see her, and bent down. "I'm sorry, kid. I got a little lost and had to find my way home."

Her lower lip trembled as tears formed in her eyes, and she threw her arms around me again. "I thought you were gone! I didn't—I didn't know—"

I touched her back with my palm. "It's okay, kid. It's okay." I cleared my throat. "I'm here, Lex. Everything's going to be all right."

"Really?" she asked, pulling away so she could see me.

I nodded. "Have I let you down yet?" I asked with a smirk. "Who're you talking to, kid?"

She giggled and hugged me again.

In the distance, I saw Alphonse, standing with one of the colonists, laughing and nodding as they talked together. He looked at me and waved. Lex and I waved back. She ran to him, while I took my time, taking in the room. There were so many people here, so many survivors. I couldn't imagine what we'd do with all of them, but I was sure we'd find a way to make this work.

As I neared Alphonse, I noticed one of the strike ships was active, its door slowly opening. Were the colonists still unloading? How many more could there be?

My eyes lingered on the ship, watching as the only

passenger began to exit, wearing a flight suit—the same one Alphonse had on.

As I continued walking toward the crowd, each of them embracing one another, I saw a face I hadn't expected.

It was Octavia, walking on two good legs, smiling at me from across the ancient bay.

EPILOGUE

THE CARGO BAY remained a mess as my crew worked on getting everyone into their own rooms. *Titan* had more than enough space to accommodate these people, so I saw no reason to keep everyone crammed into this one location.

Only a few of them remained behind to coordinate with me. Karin wanted to discuss the next step, like I had a plan or something. "I'm not sure what you want to hear," I told her. "We barely made it off that rock alive. Take a second and be glad."

Octavia had taken Lex to join Abigail, since the girl wanted to see her so badly. Alphonse, meanwhile, had stayed at my side and was observing our new friend's every word, saying nothing.

"This General Brigham person and his Union," began

Karin. "They have taken a great deal from my people. Janus was a trusted friend."

I could sense the conflict in her voice—anger, gradually replacing grief. I'd felt it many times before. "Janus did what he had to do. It was his choice. You need to learn to live with that."

She lowered her eyes to the deck. "What happens next?"

I shook my head. "I don't know. We've been lucky so far, but we can't keep running away. Eventually, one side will have to lose."

She narrowed her eyes. "It won't be us. Tell me you believe that, Captain."

"Of course he does," said Alphonse, finally speaking up. "You don't survive this long without a bit of hope."

Karin looked at me curiously. "Is that right?"

Truth was, I couldn't predict how things would go from here. I was just a Renegade from Epsy, thrown into something I didn't ask for, but I wouldn't walk away from it. I wouldn't give up everything I'd fought to keep. "We'll fight for it," I told Karin. "I don't aim to lose."

She smiled, all the doubt in her face gone. "Then you can count on the rest of us to help you."

"Are you asking me if you can stay?"

"Don't you have the room?" she asked, raising her brow.

"I'm sure we can fit you in somewhere."

Alphonse motioned at the woman's right arm. "If I

might," he began. "Your tattoos. Are they functional? Can you operate old Earth technology with them?"

Karin nodded, reaching behind her and touching the nearby strike ship. The internal lights activated. "Does that answer your question?"

Alphonse smiled. "Karin, if I might make a suggestion."

"What's that?" she asked.

The former Constable looked at me. "Captain, how many strike ships would you say are on this vessel?"

"Hard to say," I answered.

He turned to face the rest of the cargo bay, and my eyes went with him. "I think we may want to find out."

There, throughout the bay, hundreds of ships lay waiting, each one fully armed and operational. Each one, ready for combat.

All they needed were pilots.

Jace, Abigail, and Lex will return in RENEGADE FLEET, coming March 2018.

Read on for a special note from the author.

AUTHOR NOTES

I'm writing these end notes roughly two minutes after finishing the final chapter of this book, so let me just say, wow, what a fun ride.

Before I even started writing this book, I knew I wanted to tell a different kind of story from the rest of the series so far. This time, the heroes would have more than humans to contend with. There would be monsters, and they would be terrifying.

That was the idea anyway. I just wasn't sure how I'd do it. While writing *Renegade Moon*, however, all the pieces started falling into place. I've always been into genetic engineering and dystopian type societies (my first series, The Variant Saga, explores both of those concepts in-depth), so it made sense to include them here, but in a different sort of way. Given the backstory presented in *Renegade Moon* about how Lex and the other Eternals came to be, it stood to reason that, somewhere, that process could have gone wrong.

People, no matter how perfect they believe themselves to be, will always be capable of hubris. The Eternals are no different. At least, that was the general idea.

What followed was part scifi horror, part discovery. My favorite stories were always the ones that showed you "new worlds and new civilizations," took us to interesting locations, and revealed a deep, dark secret. Maybe the characters survive, maybe they don't, but there's always a puzzle to be solved, something buried in the world, and it nearly always shakes up the narrative.

In this case, we met a group of people who had built their lives on the rubble of a long dead civilization, and all they wanted was to survive. There were monsters, but as we soon discovered, they were more than they appeared.

We'll be seeing all of these characters again, along with the rest of the crew. The Union is about to come back with a vengeance, and Jace will need all the help he can get.

Until then, thanks for reading, Renegades,

JN Chaney

PS. Amazon won't tell you when the next Renegade book will come out, but there are several ways you can stay informed.

1) Fly on over to the Facebook group, JN Chaney's Renegade Readers, and say hello. It's a great place to hang with other sarcastic sci-fi readers who don't mind a good laugh.

2) Follow me directly on Amazon. To do this, head to the **store page** for this book (or my Amazon author profile) and click the Follow button beneath my picture. That will prompt Amazon to notify you when I release a new book. You'll just need to check your emails.

3) You can join my mailing list by clicking here. This will allow me to stay in touch with you directly, and you'll also receive a free copy of The Amber Project.

Doing one of these or **all three** (for best results) will ensure you know every time a new entry in *the Renegade Star series* is published. Please take a moment to do one of these so you'll be able to join Jace, Abigail, and Lex on their next galaxy-spanning adventure.

PREVIEW: THE AMBER PROJECT

Documents of Historical, Scientific, and
Cultural Significance
Play Audio Transmission File 021
Recorded April 19, 2157

CARTWRIGHT: *This is Lieutenant Colonel Felix Cartwright.*
It's been a week since my last transmission and two months since the
day we found the city…the day the world fell apart. If anyone can
hear this, please respond.

If you're out there, no doubt you know about the gas. You might
think you're all that's left. But if you're receiving this, let me assure
you, you are not alone. There are people here. Hundreds, in fact, and
for now, we're safe. If you can make it here, you will be, too.

The city's a few miles underground, not far from El Rico Air
Force Base. That's where my people came from. As always, the coordi-

nates are attached. If anyone gets this, please respond. Let us know you're there...that you're still alive.

End Audio File

April 14, 2339
Maternity District

MILES BELOW THE SURFACE OF THE EARTH, deep within the walls of the last human city, a little boy named Terry played quietly with his sister in a small two-bedroom apartment.

Today was his very first birthday. He was turning seven.

"What's a birthday?" his sister Janice asked, tugging at his shirt. She was only four years old and had recently taken to following her big brother everywhere he went. "What does it mean?"

Terry smiled, eager to explain. "Mom says when you turn seven, you get a birthday. It means you grow up and get to start school. It's a pretty big deal."

"When will I get a birthday?"

"You're only four, so you have to wait."

"I wish I was seven," she said softly, her thin black hair hanging over her eyes. "I want to go with you."

He got to his feet and began putting the toy blocks away. They had built a castle together on the floor, but

Mother would yell if they left a mess. "I'll tell you all about it when I get home. I promise, okay?"

"Okay!" she said cheerily and proceeded to help.

Right at that moment, the speaker next to the door let out a soft chime, followed by their mother's voice. "Downstairs, children," she said. "Hurry up now."

Terry took his sister's hand. "Come on, Jan," he said.

She frowned, squeezing his fingers. "Okay."

They arrived downstairs, their mother nowhere to be found.

"She's in the kitchen," Janice said, pointing at the farthest wall. "See the light-box?"

Terry looked at the locator board, although his sister's name for it worked just as well. It was a map of the entire apartment, with small lights going on and off in different colors depending on which person was in which room. *There's us*, he thought, *green for me and blue for Janice, and there's Mother in red.* Terry never understood why they needed something like that because of how small the apartment was, but every family got one, or so Mother had said.

As he entered the kitchen, his mother stood at the far counter sorting through some data on her pad. "What's that?" he asked.

"Something for work," she said. She tapped the front of the pad and placed it in her bag. "Come on, Terrance, we've got to get you ready and out the door. Today's your first day, after all, and we have to make a good impression."

"When will he be back?" asked Janice.

"Hurry up. Let's go, Terrance," she said, ignoring the question. She grabbed his hand and pulled him along. "We have about twenty minutes to get all the way to the education district. Hardly enough time at all." Her voice was sour. He had noticed it more and more lately, as the weeks went on, ever since a few months ago when that man from the school came to visit. His name was Mr. Huxley, one of the few men who Terry ever had the chance to talk to, and from the way Mother acted—she was so agitated—he must have been important.

"Terrance," his mother's voice pulled him back. "Stop moping and let's go."

Janice ran and hugged him, wrapping her little arms as far around him as she could. "Love you," she said.

"Love you, too."

"Bye," she said, shyly.

He kissed her forehead and walked to the door where his mother stood talking with the babysitter, Ms. Cartwright. "I'll only be a few hours," Mother said. "If it takes any longer, I'll message you."

"Don't worry about a thing, Mara," Ms. Cartwright assured her. "You take all the time you need."

Mother turned to him. "There you are," she said, taking his hand. "Come on, or we'll be late."

As they left the apartment, Mother's hand tugging him along, Terry tried to imagine what might happen at school today. Would it be like his home lessons? Would he be behind the other children, or was everything new? He enjoyed learning, but there was still a chance the school might be too hard for him. What would he do? Mother had taught him some things, like algebra and English, but who knew how far along the other kids were by now?

Terry walked quietly down the overcrowded corridors with an empty, troubled head. He hated this part of the district. So many people on the move, brushing against him, like clothes in an overstuffed closet.

He raised his head, nearly running into a woman and her baby. She had wrapped the child in a green and brown cloth, securing it against her chest. "Excuse me," he said, but the lady ignored him.

His mother paused and looked around. "Terrance, what are you doing? I'm over here," she said, spotting him.

"Sorry."

They waited together for the train, which was running a few minutes behind today.

"I wish they'd hurry up," said a nearby lady. She was young, about fifteen years old. "Do you think it's because of the outbreak?"

"Of course," said a much older woman. "Some of the trains are busy carrying contractors to the slums to patch the walls. It slows the others down because now they have to make more stops."

"I heard fourteen workers died. Is it true?"

"You know how the gas is," she said. "It's very quick. Thank God for the quarantine barriers."

Suddenly, there was a loud smashing sound, followed by

three long beeps. It echoed through the platform for a moment, vibrating along the walls until it was gone. Terry flinched, squeezing his mother's hand.

"Ouch," she said. "Terrance, relax."

"But the sound," he said.

"It's the contractors over there." She pointed to the other side of the tracks, far away from them. It took a moment for Terry to spot them, but once he did, it felt obvious. Four of them stood together. Their clothes were orange, with no clear distinction between their shirts and their pants, and on each of their heads was a solid red plastic hat. Three of them were holding tools, huddled against a distant wall. They were reaching inside of it, exchanging tools every once in a while, until eventually the fourth one called them to back away. As they made some room, steam rose from the hole, with a puddle of dark liquid forming at the base. The fourth contractor handled a machine several feet from the others, which had three legs and rose to his chest. He waved the other four to stand near him and pressed the pad on the machine. Together, the contractors watched as the device flashed a series of small bright lights. It only lasted a few seconds. Once it was over, they gathered close to the wall again and resumed their work.

"What are they doing?" Terry asked.

His mother looked down at him. "What? Oh, they're fixing the wall, that's all."

"Why?" he asked.

"Probably because there was a shift last night. Remember when the ground shook?"

Yeah, I remember, he thought. *It woke me up.* "So they're fixing it?"

"Yes, right." She sighed and looked around. "Where is that damned train?"

Terry tugged on her hand. "That lady over there said it's late because of the gas."

His mother looked at him. "What did you say?"

"The lady...the one right there." He pointed to the younger girl a few feet away. "She said the gas came, so that's why the trains are slow. It's because of the slums." He paused a minute. "No, wait. It's because they're *going* to the slums."

His mother stared at the girl, turning back to the tracks and saying nothing.

"Mother?" he said.

"Be quiet for a moment, Terrance."

Terry wanted to ask her what was wrong, or if he had done anything to upset her, but he knew when to stay silent. So he left it alone like she wanted. Just like a good little boy.

The sound of the arriving train filled the platform with such horrific noise that it made Terry's ears hurt. The train, still vibrating as he stepped onboard, felt like it was alive.

After a short moment, the doors closed. The train was moving.

Terry didn't know if the shaking was normal or not. Mother had taken him up to the medical wards on this train once when he was younger, but never again after that. He didn't remember much about it, except that he liked it. The medical wards were pretty close to where he lived, a few stops before the labs, and several stops before the education district. After that, the train ran through Pepper Plaza, then the food farms and Housing Districts 04 through 07 and finally the outer ring factories and the farms. As Terry stared at the route map on the side of the train wall, memorizing what he could of it, he tried to imagine all the places he could go and the things he might see. What kind of shops did the shopping plaza have, for example, and what was it like to work on the farms? Maybe one day he could go and find out for himself—ride the train all day to see everything there was to see. Boy, wouldn't that be something?

"Departure call: 22-10, education district," erupted the com in its monotone voice. It took only a moment before the train began to slow.

"That's us. Come on," said Mother. She grasped his hand, pulling him through the doors before they were fully opened.

Almost to the school, Terry thought. He felt warm suddenly. Was he getting nervous? And why now? He'd known about this forever, and it was only hitting him *now?*

He kept taking shorter breaths. He wanted to pull away and return home, but Mother's grasp was tight and firm, and the closer they got to the only major building in the area, the tighter and firmer it became.

Now that he was there, now that the time had finally come, a dozen questions ran through Terry's mind. Would the other kids like him? What if he wasn't as smart as everyone else? Would they make fun of him? He had no idea what to expect.

Terry swallowed, the lump in his throat nearly choking him.

An older man stood at the gate of the school's entrance. He dressed in an outfit that didn't resemble any of the clothes in Terry's district or even on the trains. A gray uniform—the color of the pavement, the walls, and the streets—matched his silver hair to the point where it was difficult to tell where one ended and the other began. "Ah," he said. "Mara, I see you've brought another student. I was wondering when we'd meet the next one. Glad to see you're still producing. It's been, what? Five or six years? Some-thing like that, I think."

"Yes, thank you, this is Terrance," said Mother quickly. "I was told there would be an escort." She paused, glancing over the man and through the windows. "Where's Bishop? He assured me he'd be here for this."

"The *colonel*," he corrected, "is in his office, and the boy is to be taken directly to him as soon as I have registered his arrival."

She let out a frustrated sigh. "He was supposed to meet me at the gate for this, himself. I wanted to talk to him about a few things."

"What's wrong?" Terry asked.

She looked down at him. "Oh, it's nothing, don't worry. You have to go inside now, that's all."

"You're not coming in?"

"I'm afraid not," said the man. "She's not permitted."

"It's alright," Mother said, cupping her hand over his cheek. "They'll take care of you in there."

But it's just school, Terry thought. "I'll see you tonight, though, right?"

She bent down and embraced him tightly, more than she had in a long time. He couldn't help but relax. "I'm sorry, Terrance. Please be careful up there. I know you don't understand it now, but you will eventually. Everything will be fine." She rose, releasing his hand for the first time since they left the train. "So that's it?" Mother said to the man.

"Yes, ma'am."

"Good." She turned and walked away, pausing a moment as she reached the corner and continued until she was out of sight.

The man pulled out a board with a piece of paper on it. "When you go through here, head straight to the back of the hall. A guard there will take you to see Colonel Bishop. Just do what they say and answer everything with either 'Yes, sir' or 'No, sir,' and you'll be fine. Understand?"

Terry didn't understand, but he nodded anyway.

The man pushed open the door with his arm and leg, holding it there and waiting. "Right through here you go," he said.

Terry entered, reluctantly, and the door closed quickly behind him.

The building, full of the same metal and shades of brown and gray that held together the rest of the city, rose higher than any other building Terry had ever been in. Around the room, perched walkways circled the walls, cluttered with doors and hallways that branched off into unknown regions. Along the walkways, dozens of people walked back and forth as busily as they had in the train station. More importantly, Terry quickly realized, most of them were men.

For so long, the only men he had seen were the maintenance workers who came and went or the occasional teacher who visited the children when they were nearing their birthdays. It was so rare to see any men at all, especially in such great numbers. *Maybe they're all teachers*, he thought. They weren't dressed like the workers: white coats and some with brown jackets—thick jackets with laced boots and bodies as stiff as the walls. Maybe that was what teachers wore. How could he know? He had never met one besides Mr. Huxley, and that was months ago.

"Well, don't just stand there, gawking," said a voice from the other end of the room. It was another man, dressed the same as the others. "Go on in through here." He pointed to another door, smaller than the one Terry had entered from. "Everyone today gets to meet the colonel. Go on now. Hurry up. You don't want to keep him waiting."

Terry did as the man said and stepped through the

doorway, his footsteps clanking against the hard metal floor, echoing through what sounded like the entire building.

"Well, come in, why don't you?" came a voice from inside.

Terry stepped cautiously into the room, which was much nicer than the entranceway. It was clean, at least compared to some of the other places Terry had been, including his own home. The walls held several shelves, none of which lacked for any company of things; various ornaments caught Terry's eye, like the little see-through globe on the shelf nearest to the door, which held a picture of a woman's face inside, although some of it was faded and hard to make out. There was also a crack in it. What purpose could such a thing have? Terry couldn't begin to guess. Next to it lay a frame with a small, round piece of metal inside of it. An inscription below the glass read, "U.S. Silver Dollar, circa 2064." Terry could easily read the words, but he didn't understand them. What was this thing? And why was it so important that it needed to be placed on a shelf for everyone to look at?

"I said come in," said Bishop abruptly. He sat at the far end of the room behind a large brown desk. Terry had forgotten he was even there. "I didn't mean for you to stop at the door. Come over here."

Terry hurried closer, stopping a few feet in front of the desk.

"I'm Colonel Bishop. You must be Terrance," said the man. "I've been wondering when you were going to show up." He wore a pair of thin glasses and had one of the larger pads in his hand. "Already seven. Imagine that."

"Yes, sir," Terry said, remembering the doorman's words.

The colonel was a stout man, a little wider than the others. He was older, too, Terry guessed. He may have been tall, but it was difficult to tell without seeing his whole body. "I expect you're hoping to begin your classes now," said Bishop.

"Yes, sir," he said.

"You say that, but you don't really know what you're saying yes to, do you?"

The question seemed more like a statement, so Terry didn't answer. He only stood there. Who was this man? Is this how school was supposed to be?

"Terrance, let me ask you something," said the colonel, taking a moment. "Did your mother tell you anything about this program you're going into?"

Terry thought about the question for a moment. "Um, she said you come to school on your birthday," he said. "And that it's just like it is at home, except there's more kids like me."

Colonel Bishop blinked. "That's right, I suppose. What else did she say?"

"That when it was over, I get to go back home," he said.

"And when did she say that was?"

Terry didn't answer.

Colonel Bishop cocked an eyebrow. "Well? Didn't she say?"

"No, sir," muttered Terry.

The man behind the desk started chuckling. "So you don't know how long you're here for?"

"No, sir."

Colonel Bishop set the pad in his hand down. "Son, you're here for the next ten years."

A sudden rush swelled up in Terry's chest and face. What was Bishop talking about? Of course Terry was going home. He couldn't stay here. "But I promised my sister I'd be home today," he said. "I have to go back."

"Too bad," said the colonel. "Your Mother really did you a disservice by not telling you. But don't worry. We just have to get you started." He tapped the pad on his desk, and the door opened. A cluster of footsteps filled the hall before two large men appeared, each wearing the same brown coats as the rest. "Well, that was fast," he said.

One of the men saluted. "Yes, sir. No crying with the last one. Took her right to her room without incident."

Terry wanted to ask who *the last one* was, and why it should be a good thing that she didn't cry. Did other kids cry when they came to this school? What kind of place *was* this?

"Well, hopefully Terrence here will do the same," said Bishop. He looked at Terry. "Right? You're not going to give us any trouble, are you?"

Terry didn't know what to do or what to say. All he

could think about was getting far away from here. He didn't want to go with the men. He didn't want to behave. All he wanted to do was go home.

But he couldn't, not anymore. He was here in this place with nowhere to go. No way out. He wanted to scream, to yell at the man behind the desk and his two friends, and tell them about how stupid it was for them to do what they were doing.

He opened his mouth to explain, to scream as loud as he could that he wouldn't go. But in that moment, the memory of the doorman came back to him, and instead of yelling, he repeated the words he'd been told before. "No, sir."

Bishop smiled, nodding at the two men in the doorway. "Exactly what I like to hear."

Get the Amber Project now, exclusively on Amazon

GET A FREE BOOK

Chaney posts updates, official art, previews, and other awesome stuff on his website. You can also follow him on Instagram, Facebook, and Twitter.

Search for **JN Chaney's Renegade Readers** on Facebook to join the group where readers can come together and share their lives and interests, especially regarding Chaney's books.

For updates about new releases, as well as exclusive promotions, sign up for the VIP mailing list. Head there now to receive a free copy of *The Other Side of Nowhere*.

https://www.subscribepage.com/organic

Enjoying the series? Help others discover the Variant Saga by leaving a review on Amazon.

BOOKS BY J.N. CHANEY

The Variant Saga:

The Amber Project

Transient Echoes

Hope Everlasting

The Vernal Memory

Renegade Star Series:

Renegade Star

Renegade Atlas

Renegade Moon

Renegade Lost

Renegade Fleet

Renegade Earth

Renegade Dawn

Renegade Children

Renegade Union (Jan 2019)

Renegade Empire (March 2019)

Renegade Universe:

Nameless

Orion Colony

Orion Uncharted

Orion Awakened (Jan 2019)

Standalone Books:

Their Solitary Way

The Other Side of Nowhere

ABOUT THE AUTHOR

J. N. Chaney has a Master's of Fine Arts in creative writing and fancies himself quite the Super Mario Bros. fan. When he isn't writing or gaming, you can find him online at **www.jnchaney.com**.

He migrates often but was last seen in Avon Park, Florida. Any sightings should be reported, as they are rare.

Renegade Lost is his ninth novel.

Made in the USA
Columbia, SC
12 March 2019